DEAD AMONG STARS

A MADDIE SWALLOWS MYSTERY
BOOK 4

KAT BELLEMORE

KB PRESS

CHOOSE YOUR OWN ADVENTURE: MYSTERY OR ROMANCE

MADDIE SWALLOWS MYSTERIES

Dead Before Dinner

Dead Upon Arrival

Dead Before I Do

Dead Among Stars

Dead by Design

BORROWING AMOR: New Mexican Romance

Borrowing Amor

Borrowing Love

Borrowing a Fiancé

Borrowing a Billionaire

Borrowing Kisses

Borrowing Second Chances

STARLIGHT RIDGE: Beach Romance

Diving into Love

Resisting Love

Starlight Love

Building on Love

Winning his Love

1

No one had told me how secluded the spaceport would be. It was the type of place that people only traveled to if they were looking to bury a body. I clutched the steering wheel, forcing the car to stay on the dirt road that wound its way through the desert. With every unexpected jolt, my heart followed, my anxiety increasing.

It wasn't just the drive that was rattling me.

As a psychologist, I'd found myself in a lot of interesting situations. But never something like this. Never trapped in the middle of nowhere with a bunch of celebrities. I hadn't been given a travel roster, but the rich and famous were the only ones who could afford the quarter million price tag for a two-hour trip into Earth's orbit. Apparently, the short ride into space could take a lot out of someone, both physically and mentally, and I had been hired to conduct therapy sessions with the "astronauts" as they prepared for their trip.

I was used to helping everyday people with everyday problems. The situations that came up in my therapy office, they were things that I had gone through, or I had known people who had gone through them. But someone freaking out because they had decided to go to space? That wasn't something I had experienced. How would I know what questions to ask? What if I did more harm than good? Especially because I was required to stay at the spaceport for the duration of their stay.

Four days. Three nights.

My eighteen-year-old daughter, Lilly, was supposed to be there with me as the spaceport's official photographer. That would have made things better. But when I'd poked my head into her room that morning, I'd been greeted with an empty bed and no sign of Lilly or her luggage.

The sounds of someone emptying their stomach in the toilet further down the hallway had made my heart drop.

No amount of begging could convince the spaceport to allow her to arrive a day late. They couldn't risk one of their astronauts becoming ill, and they'd been on the hunt for Lilly's replacement before I'd even left the house.

Lilly was devastated, of course. This job was supposed to be her big break, and I wished I could have stayed home with her rather than having to hurry off. As a working single mom, I always felt guilty when I couldn't be there for Lilly and her younger brother. I'd already been running late, though, so here I was, bouncing along this dirt road, wondering what in the world I was doing there.

A terrifying thought struck me. What if I was so terrible at it, they sent me packing and told me to never return?

Of course, Galactic Enterprises wouldn't ask just anyone to come on board for something so monumental. If they believed in me, surely I should believe in myself.

My downward spiral was, thankfully, interrupted when my phone burst into song. I glanced at the name that popped up on the car's dashboard screen.

My mother.

The timing couldn't be worse.

I allowed the call to go to voicemail, but then the music started up again.

Steeling myself, I pressed the answer icon on the dashboard. "Mom, I'm driving. Can we talk later?"

I'd answered the call because I'd known that if I didn't, my mother would keep calling until I finally succumbed. I immediately regretted it.

"Why are you talking while driving?" my mom asked. "You know that's the leading cause of car accidents."

I stifled a groan. "You know what? You're right. We'll talk in four days, okay?"

What looked like a guard shack appeared in the distance. Just a little further.

"That's why I'm calling, though. You never said goodbye, just up and left in the dead of night."

My mom and I had been working on our relationship since I'd moved back to my hometown of Amor, and we were making progress, but we still had our issues. And this conversation was triggering all of them. If my roommate, Trish, weren't the only other therapist in town, I'd have started seeing someone a long time ago.

"I said goodbye last night when you stopped by with food for an impromptu farewell party. A farewell party for my and Lilly's four-day absence. Why would I call you at eight this morning to tell you the exact moment I was leaving?"

A huff on the other end of the call.

"Because that's what people do when they love someone. Other daughters call their mothers. Why can't you?"

I slowed the car as I neared the guard shack. A bored-looking officer stood at a window but seemed to brighten as I stopped next to him.

"ID, please," the officer said, extending a hand.

"Who was that?" my mom's disembodied voice asked as I rummaged in my purse for my wallet. "Do you have a man in the car with you? Does Benji know?"

Just the mention of Benji made me want to turn the car around and hurry home. He'd been my best friend as long as I could remember, but when I'd moved away for college, we'd lost touch. My fault, I could admit. During the next twenty years I had managed to marry, become a professor of psychology, and raise two amazing children. And then there was the divorce and moving back to my New

Mexican hometown. That had been an unpleasant adjustment.

It had seemed the town would never forgive me for abandoning them. It wasn't their forgiveness I had cared about, though. Benji had been the only one who'd mattered.

Thankfully, it had only taken two years and solving three murders for us to realize we were meant to be together. And we had been inseparable ever since. Until today.

I ignored my mother as I produced my driver's license for the security officer. He took it from me, but then leaned forward and said through the open window, "No reason to worry, ma'am. I'm just the guy that makes sure this lovely young woman doesn't have ulterior motives for being at the spaceport today."

He smiled, like he was being funny, but I braced myself. The poor guy had no idea what he'd just done.

Silence.

And then...

"Are you implying that my granddaughter is anything other than what she presents herself to be?" my mom's voice squawked. "I'll have you know that Lilly is the best photographer this side of—"

"Lilly isn't here. She's at home, sick," I interrupted, shooting the officer an apologetic smile. This was not how I'd wanted to start my first day of work. "He was talking about me. But they're making me turn off my phone now.

See you in four days." And then I ended the call before she could say anything more.

"Sorry about that," I told the officer.

He gave a good-natured laugh, but it seemed forced as he waved me through.

My worry for the officer disappeared when I drove past the barrier and the spaceport came into view.

The pictures didn't do it justice.

A large domed building loomed in front of me. It was so big that I'd bet my university's football stadium could fit inside it. The closer I got, the more I felt like I had landed in a sci-fi movie. The domed building was nothing but windows, and the reflection of the sun made it seem like it was glowing.

I entered a gravel lot and parked the car next to a Tesla with a license plate that read ROKTMAN, and I released a low whistle. "This is...something else." I pretended my own car didn't look like something that belonged in a junkyard as I stepped out, my gaze traveling over the mani-cured gardens that surrounded the spaceport. I was impressed to see that they included native desert plants and a metal statue of a roadrunner that was nestled between two cactuses to my left.

After pulling my suitcase out of the trunk, I walked a garden path that led me past a fountain with a replica of the spacecraft that the astronauts would be flying in, and up to a pair of glass doors.

Even though I only had a couple of minutes to spare

before I'd be considered late, I paused, not yet ready to enter the building.

I had a moment of doubt—a moment when I wondered if I could do this.

But it was too late to turn back now. And there were some very rich people in need of my help. I didn't want to keep them waiting.

Sucking in a long breath, I pulled the door open. The cool air from inside washed over me, and I forced my feet to move forward.

I hoped this wasn't a mistake.

2

My pulse quickened in anticipation as I stepped into the spaceport's large entryway. Security doors were positioned at the far ends, prohibiting a sneak peek at what lay beyond, but even the area where I stood was stunning, everything streamlined, as if I had already taken my place in the spacecraft. To the right of me was a waiting area with large, plush chairs. My gaze moved up to the impossibly high ceiling, gorgeous constellations overlooking the room.

"May I help you?"

My surroundings had captured my attention so effectively that I hadn't even noticed the security officer who stood behind a desk directly in front of me.

"Maddie Swallows," I said, hurrying forward and leaning my suitcase against the desk.

The officer nodded once. "Oh, yes. You must be the one with the formidable mother."

Word traveled fast.

Heat crept into my cheeks, and I nodded. "Yes, but oddly enough, she makes a wonderful grandmother."

The officer seemed to fight a smile. "I'm sure she does." He slid a stack of papers toward me. "I'm Officer Bridge. I'll be taking care of your security clearance today. I see that you already sent in a copy of your birth certificate, social security card, and photo ID."

"I did. Seemed a bit overkill, to be honest. Never had to send in a birth certificate for a job before."

Officer Bridge's smile disappeared. "Then you've never worked for a company that is concerned about international threats. The race to space is still very real, even if it looks different than it did in the 1960s. And it's not only a race between nations, but there are multiple contenders within our own country as well. Space tourism isn't just about taking millionaires for a joy ride. Think of the practical applications—"

"All right, Officer Bridge, that's enough for now. Let's get Dr. Swallows taken care of so I can give her a lay of the land before our astronauts arrive." A woman had approached from the security doors to my right. She was petite but had a commanding presence. Not an unkind one, by any means, but she was obviously the one in charge around there.

She extended a hand toward me. "Julie Farnsworth. We

talked on the phone. You'll have to excuse Officer Bridge. He gets very excited when we discuss the possibilities that lie in the future of space tourism."

Yup. The woman in charge. Vice president of tourist relations, if I remembered correctly.

Officer Bridge dropped his gaze, mumbling as he retrieved a pen. "We require wet signatures on everything —nothing electronic will work for our purposes today. When you're finished signing these NDA forms, you'll receive your security badge."

Julie continued talking as I mindlessly signed form after form. I hoped there wasn't something hidden among the endless paperwork. For all I knew, I'd just signed over everything in my bank account, plus the deed to my house.

"I know it's a strange situation," Julie was saying. "You are going to be a part of something huge—life altering. And yet, you won't be experiencing space firsthand, and everything you do experience here in the spaceport you can't talk about. Unfair, I know. But I do hope you find it rewarding."

"How often do you have flights?" I asked, shaking out my writing hand. I still had a ways to go on the required forms, and my hand was starting to cramp up.

"We've only sent up our inaugural flight thus far. That was six months ago. We're hoping there won't be such a gap before the next flight and that we can eventually work out the efficiency kinks to where we are sending tourists up once or twice a month." She paused, and her mind suddenly seemed to be elsewhere as she said, "Nothing ever goes as planned, of course."

By the time I was finished with the seemingly endless stack of forms, my security badge was already attached to a lanyard and I was ready to go.

Julie glanced at her phone. "We have time for a quick tour before our guests arrive. I hope you don't mind if Jeffrey joins us."

"Jeffrey?" I had no idea who the man was but didn't see why that would be a problem.

Julie looked puzzled. "I'm sorry, I thought you two knew each other. He's the photographer from your town that we had to bring in last minute. We were lucky he was available and that he could get out here so quickly. Though I must say that losing Lilly was a terrible blow. Please let her know that we wish her a speedy recovery."

I nodded and said I would, but my thoughts were spinning. There was another decent photographer in Amor? The pickings were pretty slim, which was why Lilly had always stood out. Not that she wouldn't have stood out against stiffer competition, but it did make it easier. The only other person in town who even pretended they knew what to do with a camera was—

Oh, no.

"You don't mean Jeffrey Monroe."

Julie's expression brightened. "Oh, you do know him. There will be no need for introductions, then. He's just using the restroom, and then we can begin."

I didn't know who Julie had talked to, but whoever had recommended Jeffrey had to be out of their mind. It was probably his mother. If I remembered correctly, she had some connection to the tourist industry. I wondered if I should mention that Jeffrey had been hired to be the photographer at a wedding last summer and hadn't realized he'd forgotten to remove the lens cap until halfway through the event.

That hadn't been a good day for either the happy couple or the town of Amor, considering we'd had to hear about the disaster for weeks afterwards.

I glanced Jeffrey's way as he exited the bathroom and hoped for his sake that he'd learned his lesson last summer.

"Great, we can begin," Julie said.

Jeffrey beamed as he nodded to me in greeting. He was lanky, a camera hanging from his neck. Freckles covered every visible part of him, and when he gave me a toothy grin, the freckles seemed to multiply. This had to be the best thing that had happened to him in his short twenty-three years, and he looked so happy, I prayed there wouldn't be any disasters.

And under no circumstances could Lilly find out that this was who had been chosen to take her place.

"Jeffrey, you'll be stationed outside the spaceport when the astronauts arrive." Julie nodded toward the front of the building. "You are expected to document the astronauts' entire journey, from their first day to their last."

Jeffrey half-raised his hand, as if he were back in school. "But they aren't astronauts. Not really."

I cringed, knowing that contradicting your supervisor wasn't the best way to start things at your new job. Especially when you weren't their first choice. Did I think it a bit corny that they referred to the millionaires who wanted a joyride to space astronauts? Yes. But I wasn't going to be the one to say anything.

"Have you ever been to space?" Julie asked, her lips pursed. "Have you ever seen the curvature of the Earth while you mingle among the stars?"

Jeffrey shook his head, shrinking under her gaze.

"If our own former astronaut, Dr. Randall, is okay with it, then you should probably get used to the idea." Her expression softened. "The guests will receive one framed photo as a memento of their flight, and the rest will be used for promotional purposes. The one area you are not allowed to enter is the astronauts' dormitories, but you will be able to access every other area they have clearance for." Julie took a step forward. "You are to be everywhere, and yet remain invisible. You are never to ask a guest to pose, and you are never to interfere with their activities. With the exception of the official photograph of them in their space suits on launch day, every photo will be taken discreetly. And they all belong to the spaceport. You will not retain any pictures for your own personal use. Do you understand?"

Jeffrey seemed a bit taken aback by the urgency in

Julie's tone, his eyes wide, but he nodded and managed a "Yes, ma'am."

Julie smiled and stepped back, straightening her blouse as she did so. "Wonderful." She then turned her attention to me, and I swallowed hard, worried what instructions I might receive. "Let's begin the tour, shall we?"

Looked like the vice president of tourist relations was saving my lecture for later. I was unsure if I should be worried by that.

"Let's try your badges on this door," she said as she turned to her right and walked briskly toward the set of locked doors.

Jeffrey lifted the badge around his neck and swiped it over a gray box positioned next to the door. A click could be heard, and Julie pulled the door open.

"Welcome to a whole new world," she said, ushering us through the doorway.

I was unsure what I had expected the inner workings of the spaceport to look like. Something that mirrored the otherworldly feeling I'd experienced when I'd first arrived, perhaps. Or maybe something reminiscent of *Star Trek* or *Star Wars*. Something that made me feel like I was about to embark on an adventure.

I was left disappointed.

Jeffrey and I were led down an ordinary hallway with cream walls and fluorescent lighting. I wanted to double check to make sure a prank wasn't being pulled on us.

That we weren't, in fact, being brought in for a routine doctor's exam, or a dental cleaning. Nothing could have been less impressive than the rows of offices we were being paraded past.

"I know what you're thinking," Julie said. "We've spent billions to provide the opportunity for the average person to travel to space, and we can't afford better decorations." She laughed at her own joke. "Not to worry, though. It will look quite different when you are here for our next flight. Our priority has been the areas that are customer facing. The rest will follow."

My thoughts stuck on Julie saying the average person had the opportunity to travel to space. I certainly couldn't afford a flight, and I was as average as they came.

Unlike Jeffrey, I kept my thoughts to myself. Despite my warning looks, begging him not to say anything, he was unable to contain himself.

"If making flights accessible to everyone really is your goal," he said, "do you foresee a time when a ticket will cost less than its current price tag of a quarter of a million dollars?"

He didn't sound like he was trying to be offensive—it was a genuine question—and I tried not to show how interested I was in the answer.

Julie hesitated. "Because of some unforeseen circumstances in the development of our spacecraft, the price per ticket was recently raised to four hundred and fifty thousand dollars. It is space, after all."

My breath caught in my chest. Half a million dollars. For a vacation for one.

Jeffrey's eyebrows shot up. "Seems that even many millionaires will be unable to afford a trip with you, let alone someone who is...average."

Julie gave him a pacifying smile. "We're working on that." She gestured to the hallway we'd been walking. "These are administrative offices. You shouldn't have the need to come here often, but in case of an emergency, we have given you access. Not to worry, Dr. Swallows, your office is in another section of the spaceport. The nice part."

The next thirty minutes passed in a blur, and I had no idea how I was going to remember where anything was. Jeffrey clicked away on his camera as we were shown a variety of conference rooms, a gymnasium, a training pool, recreation rooms for downtime, a life-size simulator of the spacecraft, and my personal favorite, the cafeteria.

"Do you take credit cards?" I asked, eyeing the buffet that took up the entire length of the room. There was everything a girl could hope for within those four walls. Mexican food, made-to-order pizza, all of my favorite Thai foods, a salad bar and Mongolian barbecue...maybe I'd just move in. It didn't hurt that the ginormous area was completely decked out with rockets hanging from the ceiling, stars littering the walls, and a glowing moon casting a cheerful glow across the room.

"No, we don't," Julie said, seeming amused at my reaction. Her eyes were bright, and I could tell she was trying not to laugh. "Everything in here is free. Because you are unable to leave the spaceport for the duration of our astronauts' stay, we figure it's only fair that we feed you."

This was where I was meant to be.

"Don't tell Flash, or we'll never hear the end of it," Jeffrey told me.

Oh, Flash. My teenage son would be in heaven. His world revolved around food, and if Flash ever got the chance to see this, he'd never leave. Literally. He'd set up camp, and security would have to haul him away.

Flash must have gained quite the reputation in the short time we'd lived in Amor if even Jeffrey Monroe knew about his food obsession. Judging by my reaction to the cafeteria, he'd inherited that obsession from me.

"Lunch is eleven to two. Dinner is four to seven. Snacks are available all day," Julie said. She glanced at her phone. She did that a lot. "I hate to hurry you along, but our astronauts will be arriving in twenty minutes." Julie turned on her heel and hurried out the cafeteria doors.

I threw a parting glance at the buffet as Jeffrey said, "Pretty sure we're supposed to follow her."

"I know." Disappointment tinged my words, and I hurried out after Julie. Because I was a mature adult. One with a PhD. A professional. And I was not ruled by a gremlin in my hypothalamus. Just because my cannabinoid receptors were currently going crazy didn't mean I needed to vault over the buffet table and grab everything I could stuff in my mouth before being escorted off the premises.

Lies, my stomach whispered to me.

"You only have to wait two hours," Jeffrey said with a smirk as we hurried down the hallway. I paused, looking in each direction. Somehow we'd already managed to lose Julie and get ourselves lost in the process. Not a great way to start the day.

Just when I was ready to yell out "Marco" and hope Julie knew enough to respond with "Polo," she appeared around a corner to our left. "Your office is down here, Dr. Swallows."

"You can call me Maddie," I said.

"All right, Maddie." Julie motioned for me to join her.

After my immediate obsession with the cafeteria, I didn't expect any other room in the spaceport to be able to steal my breath.

Until I entered my office. The lights were dim, and the way the walls were painted, it felt like I'd stepped into Van Gogh's *The Starry Night*.

"This is amazing," I said, immediately beginning a mental checklist of ways I needed to improve my office back in Amor. Compared to this, my office was sterile— something that belonged in a prison.

"We want our astronauts to feel comfortable talking about anything that might be worrying them and catch any red flags in regard to their mental health. They will essentially be trapped in a capsule, hurtling through the

Earth's atmosphere, after all. Can't have anyone going crazy."

That was a terrifying thought.

Julie clapped her hands together. "So, let's go meet our astronauts."

3

A shuttle pulled up in front of the spaceport, and I nervously waited next to the security desk, craning my neck in an attempt to catch a glimpse of the astronauts through the glass front doors. Jeffrey stood outside, already snapping photos, though no one had emerged from the vehicle yet. I really hoped he'd remembered to remove the lens cap.

"Nervous?" Officer Bridge asked. He was older than me, his hair graying on the sides. Now that all my forms had been signed, he seemed more relaxed and offered me a kind smile.

I released a small laugh. "Yes, though I have no idea why. I don't keep up on the latest celebrity news, so I doubt I'll even know who any of the astronauts are. They'll just be another patient in my office—you know, if my office back home looked like we were about to jump to warp speed and travel across space."

Officer Bridge lowered his voice to a conspiratorial whisper as Julie welcomed the guests and escorted them into the spaceport. "Don't let any of them hear you say that. Most people who can afford these flights like to be appreciated—and recognized."

"They don't get tired of that?" I asked, genuinely perplexed. "People always wanting to snap pictures and demanding autographs in random—and not always appropriate—places?"

Officer Bridge's attention shifted away from me and toward the large group moving toward the desk. He straightened several already-straight piles of papers and then launched into a speech about safety protocols and the importance of always having their security badge while on the premises.

I moved away from the desk, unsure if Julie would be introducing me to the astronauts or if I'd meet them later. For now, I'd use the opportunity to study them. A lot could be learned when someone didn't realize they were being watched. Granted, these celebrities were used to having all eyes on them, and they likely slipped into their public personas every time they left the house.

Even now, Jeffrey was walking the room, snapping pictures, and they didn't even glance his way.

I doubted they could fake every interaction, though. I

considered a man who stood near the front. He was too handsome for his own good, chiseled jaw and perfect hair included. A pretty but short woman stood behind him and was weaving side to side, trying to get a better view. I watched as the man glanced behind him, noticed the predicament, then stepped back to allow her to move closer.

She nodded in gratitude.

Whoever the man was, he had an air of confidence, but at the same time, humility.

Unlike the slightly less charming man to his left. Officer Bridge had just asked the astronauts to fill out the additional paperwork, and the man jostled his way to the front, stepping on the short woman's toes in the process.

She jumped back to get out of his way and ended up colliding with an older woman and someone who appeared to be her daughter, if their corresponding outfits were anything to go by. The mother exuded elegance. It wasn't only her clothing, which I was certain cost more than my entire wardrobe put together, but the way she held herself. The straight back and chin that tilted up. Her smooth movements. She frowned as she adjusted her flowered blouse. Her daughter, on the other hand, sent a volley of curse words at the short woman.

A young man wearing a newsboy cap leaned against the end of the security counter, looking bored, like he couldn't wait to get this over with. He wore a Zelda T-shirt, and I had no doubt he'd rather be in a dark basement with his video games than here, forced to be out among society.

You'd think that for half a million dollars, he might show at least a little interest in what was going on around him.

I did a mental head count of the group. Six astronauts. I'd sworn there were meant to be seven. I recounted. Still six.

It was then I noticed a seventh guest who stood on the periphery of the group. She had blonde curly hair that billowed around her, and she wore a small smile, as if she were amused by everything going on around her. But also like she wasn't a part of it. Like she was only there to observe.

Seeing the dynamic between everyone made me realize how glad I was that I'd be meeting with them one on one and that it would be for a limited time each day.

Julie walked up beside me. "You ready for a challenge?"

I blew out a hard breath. "I'll do my best."

She smiled. "I'm not asking you to change anyone's life here. Just get them through the next four days relatively unscathed. They'll each be scheduled for a forty-five-minute session between today and tomorrow. If they would like to schedule more sessions with you, they are able to see you as often as they would like. In our inaugural group, we saw a lot of panic attacks, and we want to provide the needed support. But your most important sessions will be after their flight. It's the real reason we decided we needed to bring a psychologist on board."

I raised an eyebrow. "I don't understand why. They've already made it through the experience."

"One of the surprising effects of going to space is re-evaluating life choices." Julie's gaze scanned the group in front of us. They didn't seem to be used to having to wait for anything, still jostling to see who could get their paper-work first. "Seeing the Earth from above—it changes a person. And sometimes that can freak a person out. Some-times they start to question things. Have regrets. We want you here to help them through that."

No pressure or anything.

"I thought you said you weren't asking me to change anyone's life."

Julie folded her arms across her chest and turned toward me. "You're here as a guide. What they do with this experience is up to them."

The mother and daughter duo received their security badges and stepped away, allowing the short woman to finally push her way through to the counter and retrieve her paperwork.

"Of course, some people can't be helped. At the very least, though, we can make sure they don't leave here trau-matized. If they don't come back from space wearing a smile and gushing about the flight to their friends, we've done something wrong."

Guide them through a life-changing experience. No trauma. Lots of smiles.

It may only be four days, but I had a feeling I was going to need a vacation after this.

. . .

I HAD two hours before my first session. Long enough for the astronauts to have a last-minute medical examination and go through orientation.

And I knew exactly what I was going to do with that time.

Study.

I wanted to know who these people were before they stepped into my office.

Except, I had no idea where I was going. It felt like days since Julie had taken Jeffrey and me on our tour, rather than the sixty minutes it had been, and I soon found myself turned around.

After my third wrong turn, I stumbled across Jeffrey in a side hallway. "Thank goodness," I said. "You'd think they'd have handed out a map or something. I need your help."

Jeffrey chuckled and walked over, his camera swinging from his neck. "You're looking for the cafeteria, aren't you?"

Ooh, that did sound good. Eat first, then study.

"Maybe," I said, the word coming out slowly. "And my office. Julie sent over files on the guests so I would at least be somewhat acquainted with their backgrounds. Do you know which way I go from here?"

Jeffrey threw a glance behind him at one of the side doors. "Sorry, I just follow the astronauts. I wouldn't be able to find my way out of this labyrinth if a lifetime supply of pizza depended on it."

Well, that just wouldn't do. At this rate, I was going to lose my job, or worse, starve.

"Anything interesting so far?" I asked.

Jeffrey's voice dropped to a whisper. "It's like front row seats to the best show in town. From what I can tell, everyone knows everyone else. And not all of them are happy about being here together."

"I see."

Jeffrey gave a solemn nod. "Especially Charlotte Fischer." My confusion must have been evident because he looked at me in shock. "The fashion icon?"

Nope, still no bells.

He shook his head, like he didn't know how I'd made it through life without this vital piece of information. "The lady with the hair piled on top of her head and the loose, flowery clothes that are worth more than our lives?"

Oh, the elegant mother.

"Got it." I gave him a thumbs up.

He gave me his signature smirk as he continued. "You turn on the news, and she's there. She's legendary. Don't expect her to open up in your little therapy sessions, though. Charlotte seems to have placed herself and her daughter, Emma, on a different plane than her fellow travelers. And she expects to be treated as such."

I bristled at his words. It was as if he thought I was here to play pretend or dress up. "I'm here for them, not the other way around." I glanced at the time on my phone. "If they don't want to open up and would rather sit for forty-five minutes in silence, that's fine by me. But my patients back home never make it more than ten before they start talking, just to ease the silence."

Jeffrey raised a shoulder. "They might talk, but don't expect it to mirror reality. These people live in a fantasy world."

That may be true, but at times, their reality seemed like fantasy to me. They were preparing for a two-hour trip to space, after all.

The door to our left burst open, and a distinguished-looking man strode out, his lips pulled into a frown. "This group has a much different dynamic than the last," he muttered. His gaze landed on Jeffrey and me, and his expression opened in surprise. "Oh, I'm sorry. I didn't realize anyone was out here."

I smiled and extended a hand. "Maddie Swallows. Resident psychologist."

The man took my hand in his. "Dr. Swallows, then, is it? I'm Dr. Frederick Randall." He released my hand and glanced over his shoulder. "You'll have your hands full with these ones. I'm not sure what's going on, but there's an undercurrent I can't quite place a finger on."

"I noticed something similar when they were checking in with Officer Bridge," I said, "but if I'm not mistaken, your inaugural group that came six months ago had some work to do before they became a cohesive group as well."

Dr. Randall looked perplexed at how I could possibly know this, but then his expression cleared. "That's right, two of our astronauts are from your town. Bev Miller and Katie Freedman." He lifted a shoulder. "I suppose you're right. These folks just need a little time in the centrifuge, and they'll be right as rain."

Centrifuge. I wasn't familiar with it. Another thing I'd need to look up.

The astronauts began to file out of the room, and Dr. Randall glanced back, a sudden anxious look crossing his features. "Lunch break," he said, before hurrying off.

Charlotte and her daughter were the first to exit, and Jeffrey lifted his camera to take pictures.

It didn't escape Charlotte's attention. "Must you do that?" she asked, wrinkling her nose in displeasure. "Everywhere we go, there you are. I get enough of that at home, and this is meant to be a vacation."

"Leave the poor photographer alone," someone said. It was the woman who had been standing at the edge of the group earlier. "He's just doing his job. And we receive some of the photos to remember the experience by. I'd think you'd be happy they'll have lots to choose from."

Charlotte didn't turn to face the woman, her features hardening. "For some of us, it only takes one try to get the perfect shot."

"Come now, ladies," the chiseled-jawed man said, slinging an arm around Charlotte's shoulders. "We're here for the experience of a lifetime." His voice dropped to a low whisper. "We're going to space." He then dramatically stared off into the distance. Definitely an actor.

Charlotte shrugged his arm off with an air of disproval. "Come on, Emma. I need a smoke."

She'd need to leave the spaceport to do that.

Charlotte's daughter followed her out a side door, but not without a backward glance, like she wished she could spend time with the others.

Emma. I'd have to look at her file. The way she held herself, she seemed to have plenty of confidence in her place in the world, but she hadn't said a word, that I'd noticed, since she'd arrived. Always in her mother's gigantic shadow.

I looked forward to our session.

THERAPY NOTES

Rachel Sinclair:

A lovely woman. She was the short one I'd noticed earlier. Easily overlooked. When I mentioned the incident that had occurred at the security desk earlier, she admitted that it wasn't the first time she'd been stepped on, and it wouldn't be the last. People don't tend to notice her.

Except the good-looking actor who had shifted out of the way for her.

Her expression brightened at the memory. Ace Hutchins, I learned was his name. I've always been terrible at knowing who celebrities are, but I may need to make more of an effort if they allow me to continue this job.

Note to self: Ask Lilly to educate me on celebrity news and culture.

Apparently, Rachel is a well-known singer, and when on stage, all eyes are on her. She claims that's enough. When off stage, she's able to lead a somewhat normal life, because people just don't take notice.

I'm not sure I believe that this doesn't bother her, but she seems to have convinced herself of its truthfulness. I hope I'm able to get to know her better.

She's excited about the prospect of going to space, though she did say that at first, she dreaded coming. Kept thinking about worst-case scenarios. Now that she's here, she's glad she followed through.

She smiled when she said this, but her focus didn't seem to be on me. Maybe there's a specific reason she's happy she's here.

Like maybe a handsome man with a chiseled jaw?

Ace Hutchins:

I was right. The chiseled-jawed man is an actor. From what I've seen, he's kind, conscientious, and not at all what I would expect from someone with his success. He tells me he's what the industry calls an A-list actor. I didn't realize there are lists for these kinds of things and asked him to explain. Basically, he's never out of a job. Everyone wants him in their films, and he can be choosy about what he wants to do. Sounds pretty cushy to me.

In spite of Ace's good manners, I have a feeling he's not being completely open with me. I asked if he knows the other astro-nauts, and he mentioned his best friend is here. Whitney Beaumont.

When I asked about the others in the group, he sort of clammed up. I have a feeling there's some bad blood somewhere in the mix, but he's too nice a guy to bring it up. Or, more likely, it's because he knows I'll be talking to the others as well.

I'd never mention anything about our conversation, of course. Patient confidentiality and all that. Hopefully if the pressure gets to be too much, he'll return for another session, though it's doubtful. He's one of the ones who puts on a good show and exudes more confidence than anyone has the right to have—but still, you never know.

Whitney Beaumont:

What a curious man. He did confirm that he and Ace had originally decided to come on the space flight together, but anytime his friend was mentioned, Whitney's expression clouded. As if there is trouble in paradise, and either Ace doesn't know it or he's very good at hiding it.

When I tried to dig deeper, Whitney shut me out. Said he didn't feel like talking and considered the possibility that coming to the spaceport had been a mistake. Said he feels claustrophobic, trapped with all these people twenty-four hours a day, never able to escape. He's only been here five hours.

His gaze darted over the room throughout the session, as if he were looking for a way out.

The room that had calmed others, and me, seemed to have the opposite effect on him. No number of stars littered throughout the room would have been enough. If anything, they seemed to aggravate him.

One aspect of my job is to report any astronaut that seems to be struggling with their mental health. The training exercises *don't only test the astronauts physically, but mentally as well. Here at the spaceport, they follow the doctor's creed of "Do no harm," and I'm wondering if I need to report my concerns. I can't reveal specific details from the session, of course, but I can ask them to keep a close eye on him. Make sure he's okay.*

I'm just not sure that being literally trapped inside a space-craft, hurtling toward space, is the best place for him.

Charlotte Fischer:

Jeffrey was right. Charlotte is a fashion icon, and she is very aware of just how legendary she is. She doesn't deal with men's fashion, strictly women. She says it takes no imagination to dress a man, and that frankly, they don't appreciate her talent.

But Charlotte won't put her dresses on just anybody. They have to be vetted first.

Curious, I asked what her criteria was, and she snorted. "There is no criteria. I just know."

Even though Charlotte and I were together for the full forty-five minutes, I don't know this woman any more than I did the moment she walked in. I can say with some certainty, however, that she has a God complex. She claims that every woman who has won an Oscar or a Grammy for the past seven years was wearing one of her dresses. I don't know if she thinks her dresses wield such power that they give the wearer an extra advantage over their competitors or if she just thinks her perception and judgment of who to work with are flawless.

Either way, when asked if she would consider working with the women in their group at the spaceport, she almost seemed angry. She said she wouldn't work with any of them, her own daughter included.

Poor girl. I'll be meeting with her next. She and I might have a lot to work with. It can't be easy having a mother like Charlotte.

Emma Fischer:

I was wrong when I said Emma and I would have a lot to talk about. It was difficult to get her to talk at all. She seems so used to standing quietly in the background that she no longer has the ability to have her own thoughts. When I asked why she chose to go to space, she said her mother had purchased the ticket for her. Charlotte hadn't even ask Emma if she was interested in going. That had been several years earlier, and they'd been waiting for Galactic Enterprises to complete the spacecraft ever since.

She doesn't resent her mother, from what I can tell, and instead puts her on a pedestal.

Emma says she's an artist, and she's living at home while she's building her career. I try not to make assumptions about my patients, but her mother seems to be in no hurry to push her twenty-four-year-old daughter out of the nest.

This puts Emma far more under her mother's influence because she's reliant on her. Charlotte has more money than any one person can spend in a lifetime, and Emma lives off those riches. Charlotte provides financial security, and Emma provides her mother with....what? I don't think companionship is what Charlotte is after. Control, maybe?

Either way, it appears to be an unhealthy relationship. If they refuse to see it—or don't want to—there's not much I can do in one session. Or in a lifetime of sessions.

Serena Barre:

The mysterious woman with beautifully wild curls. I'm not sure if anyone knows what Serena's real name is, as the one in her file was a name she'd given herself. I guess that's common in the psychic world, or so she tells me.

When she'd interacted with the group earlier, I hadn't noticed anything different about her. Maybe she liked to stand back and observe a little more than the others, but that's not unusual in a foreign situation. What is unusual is a patient trying to give me a palm reading in the middle of a session. She was taken aback when I declined. Offended, even.

Serena tells me she's the premier psychic in LA. All the celebrities apparently use her, though her whole countenance dropped when she told me they'd never admit to it in public. It's more of a hush-hush kind of thing, even though she's helped advance many of their careers with her predictions.

She must be doing quite well for herself if she could afford half a million dollars for this flight.

The rest of the session was her predicting death and destruction, though she wouldn't tell me who, where, or how. That seems pretty par for the course with these psychic types.

What is she doing here?

Noah:

There is no info on this guy. No background. No last name. He obviously enjoys video games, considering his attire. Not sure what the newsboy cap says about him. He didn't say a word during the entire forty-five minutes, and merely munched on candy bars and emptied energy drinks the entire time. He literally brought in a plastic bag of the stuff, just so he'd have something to do during our session. Wouldn't even look at me. It was like I wasn't there.

I know nothing about Noah and have no idea why he's here or if he's mentally fit to go through the rigorous training.

Maybe I should mention this one to Julie?

4

It was on the second day that I once again got lost. This time I stumbled upon the entire group as they sat on chairs in an otherwise deserted hallway, as if they were waiting for something. A spaceport employee stood nearby, stretching her calves against the wall. Jeffrey was to her right, camera in hand, looking ready to pounce if anything remotely interesting happened.

I knew I wasn't supposed to directly approach the astronauts outside of our therapy sessions, but no one had said I couldn't speak with employees who just happened to be standing in their vicinity.

"Hi," I said, approaching the woman.

She jumped, looking startled, but then her expression cleared and she smiled. "You must be the famous Dr. Swallows I keep hearing about. I'm Lori." She extended a hand. "I'm the medical officer here."

Whatever the astronauts were waiting for required medical personnel standing by. That was not something I'd want to be a part of.

"I got turned around. Again," I told her, giving her a sheepish smile.

"Every time," Whitney spoke up from our left. "I can't get one hallway correct."

Ace laughed and gave his friend a playful punch on the shoulder. "You can't get the hallways right at home. How did you think you were going to manage here?"

Whitney smiled, but it didn't reach his eyes. In fact, unless I was mistaken, those eyes were filled with contempt for his so-called friend. "I'm not the only one who has gotten turned around here."

"I don't have any trouble with it," Serena said. "But then again, I do have the gift, so I'm sure that helps."

Rachel scrunched up her nose. "I don't understand your gift. My friends say you have the ability to make predictions and guide them when they're unsure if they should accept or turn down opportunities. But you can't really see the future, can you? I mean, you're wrong sometimes. Like when you told Whitney a couple of years back to turn down the role of—"

"It was a good decision," Whitney snapped.

Judging by his intense reaction, it hadn't been, but he was trying to save face in front of people he clearly saw as rivals.

Rachel was oblivious, though, and pushed on. "Ace was

hired for the role instead, and it was what launched his career."

Whitney spluttered. "If I hadn't turned it down, I wouldn't be—"

"The amazing B-list actor that you are?" Charlotte asked, a corner of her lips pulling into an amused smile. "Playing second fiddle to Ace Hutchins?"

She was fueling the fire, and she knew it.

Whitney's whole body tensed, and Ace placed a hand on his shoulder, keeping him seated.

"It's not true, and you know it, so calm down," he said in a low voice. "Don't let her get to you."

Whitney's breaths were coming fast. He believed it was true. Every word of it.

But anything he might have said or done was forestalled when Dr. Randall pushed through a door to our right, Emma leaning on him for support.

"She'll need some crackers and juice," he told Lori, "but she did wonderfully."

Emma gave a weak smile and collapsed into the chair closest to the medical officer.

The rest of the astronauts looked as concerned as I felt, but their concern seemed to be more for themselves than for Emma. I didn't blame them.

"What is in that room?" I asked, unable to help myself. What kind of tests were they putting these people through?

Dr. Randall turned a smile on me. "The centrifuge. But

no worries, no one has died yet."

His joke fell flat and only increased the tension that had already enveloped the astronauts.

"I'll show you it later," he assured me, then cleared his throat and returned his attention to the astronauts. "Noah. I believe you're next."

Noah glanced up from where he sat, his chair tilted so it was balanced on the back two legs. "No, thank you."

Dr. Randall studied Noah for a moment. "It would be beneficial to learn these techniques before we launch in two days. You think you know what to expect but—"

"No. Thank you," Noah repeated.

Dr. Randall was quiet for another moment before nodding, and turned to Charlotte. "I guess that means it's your turn."

As Charlotte stood, she threw a glare Noah's way. Before she reached the door, however, Serena rushed forward and took Charlotte's hands in hers.

Everyone stared. No one approached Charlotte like that. Ever. Charlotte was at a loss of words and appeared too stunned to remove her hands from Serena's grasp.

Serena had always been so calm and nonplussed when I'd seen her. But this version of her—gripping Charlotte tightly, her gaze intense—was unnerving.

"The world is going to miss you, Charlotte. It will be a great loss to us all."

Charlotte snapped out of her daze and pushed Serena away. "How dare you? By the time we get out of this place,

I'm going to make sure you never work again. You quack."
And then she spun away and disappeared into the room
that housed this mysterious centrifuge.

"Not a smart move," Rachel said to Serena. "You've
angered the gods."

Serena's gaze flittered around the faces staring at her
and then to her vacated seat, almost as if she were
confused how she'd gotten there. "I don't understand."

"You know, predicting that Charlotte is going to die on
the centrifuge," Whitney said, nodding toward the door.
"When she comes out, you might not want to stick
around."

Serena sat back down. "But I didn't do anything of the
sort."

"I'm sorry, but you did," Ace said, giving her an apologetic smile.

When Charlotte exited the room twelve minutes later,
Serena took one look at her and promptly offered to show
me the way back to my office.

As we walked, I hesitated to strike up a conversation—I
was unsure if I was allowed. But walking in silence became
unbearably awkward, and I took the risk.

"When did you know you had a gift?" I asked her.
"That you were different from others."

Serena's anxious expression that had persisted since
her premonition finally cleared, and her eyes lit up. "I was
twelve," she said.

I couldn't hide my surprise. "So young?"

She gave a single nod as she led me around a corner. "I was sitting at home, reading a book, when I had the distinct feeling that I needed to tell our housekeeper she needed to return home at once—that something terrible had happened to her husband." She gave a little laugh. "Our housekeeper thought I was just trying to get rid of her so I could sneak out and go to a friend's house, and in all honesty, that's exactly what I did. But the premonition had been real—the universe's energy had communicated with me. I learned to trust those feelings."

Serena stopped halfway down the hallway, and I realized I was already back at my office. "What happened to the husband?" I asked.

She grinned. "He'd fallen asleep on his tractor and ran straight through a fence into the pigpen. Took the rest of the day to round them up."

She gave me a little wave, then I watched as she jogged back the way we'd come, likely trying to make it back in time for her turn on the centrifuge.

If I were her, I'd take my sweet time. The centrifuge was nothing I'd want to rush back for.

But then again, as a psychic, maybe she knew something that I didn't.

LATER THAT MORNING, I was between sessions when my phone rang and Benji's face popped up. I couldn't stop the teenage-girl grin from erupting over my face.

Even though I'd known Benji my whole life, a few months earlier something had clicked, and now he wasn't just my best friend—he was my everything. There wasn't a day that went by we didn't see each other, cook together, talk together—and this trip out to the spaceport was killing me. I'd never thought as a middle-aged woman I'd be able to feel like this again.

"Benji," I half-yelled when I answered the phone. "I miss you!"

Laughter on the other end. "Right back at ya. I know it's only been twenty-four hours, but I have half a mind to storm the spaceport and whisk you back home. Then again, you might not want me to, considering the celebrities you're surrounded by. How is it? Amazing?"

I hesitated too long.

"What's wrong?"

"Nothing," I quickly said. "It's just...different than I was expecting. I thought I'd be doing some good here, but no one seems to want my help. They talk to me out of obligation, but it seems more of a chance for the astronauts to reaffirm their own importance. Honestly, being whisked back home doesn't sound so bad right now."

"I bet you're doing more good than you realize," Benji said. "In fact—"

My focus was pulled away by a knock at the door. Strange. I wasn't expecting anyone for another hour and had actually been about to leave for lunch.

I stood and opened my office door as Benji continued his pep talk.

Noah waited on the other side.

"Hey, hon. Sorry, I'm going to have to let you go," I told Benji. "Call me tonight, okay?"

After a quick goodbye, I slipped the phone into my back pocket. "Noah, what can I do for you?"

He lifted a bag of candy bars and energy drinks, as if that should be answer enough. He was there for a therapy session, though I was unsure why. I opened the door wider, allowing Noah to pass me.

Once again, he didn't say a word the entire time he was there. Though he did offer me some of his snacks, which I readily accepted. They'd help tide me over until I could make it to some real food.

My watch beeped at the end of the hour, and I asked Noah if he'd like to set up a session for the next day. He nodded, and we set it up for the same time.

Maybe Benji was right. It was possible I was making a difference without realizing it. Why else would Noah come back? The only other astronaut who had voluntarily returned was Serena. She'd said it was because there had been a lot of in-fighting among the astronauts, and their negative energy was interfering with her abilities. Her vision had become clouded.

I thought it had more to do with avoiding Charlotte after the centrifuge incident.

The next day, before Noah's appointment, I made sure I

came prepared. A few minutes before we were set to meet, I grabbed a tray from the cafeteria and was surprised to see that Noah was doing the same. In some ways, I felt like there was an unspoken connection between Noah and me, though what it meant, I was unsure.

When Noah arrived at my office, he was sans candy and energy drinks and instead brought huevos rancheros, one of my favorites—fried eggs on corn tortillas, smothered with a green chile sauce and cheese, with a warmed tortilla on the side.

Didn't get better than that.

I had opted for the pad Thai.

We were twenty minutes into the session when Noah spoke. It surprised me so much, I choked on a bite of noodles and made a frantic grab for my water bottle.

"I don't want to go on the flight tomorrow."

I waited for him to continue, but he didn't.

"It's normal to have the jitters before doing something new—something unknown. Up until now, everything you've done has been training—simulations. It's quite a different thing to be hurtling through space." Then I remembered he'd opted out of the training exercises. I would be nervous too.

He seemed to think on that as he chewed.

"I'm not scared," he finally said. "I just don't want to go. There are other things I'd rather be doing. These past few days, I think I got a pretty good feeling for what it will be like. I went on the simulator yesterday afternoon. It was required. Now that I've had the experience, I'm ready to go home."

I took a bite of pad Thai to give me time to think. Physically going to space didn't matter to him. The experience of knowing what it would be like was enough. I sometimes wished I was more like that—driven by experiencing life rather than the accomplishments I could wear for everyone to see. Except, he hadn't experienced everything.

"You know what certain parts of it will be like," I said. "But you haven't experienced microgravity—what it's like to float. You haven't seen the Earth from a distance, everything so small and inconsequential."

Noah ate from his tray, silent for several minutes. I'd thought he'd finished talking for the day when his gaze met mine.

"I know what Earth looks like. And trust me when I say, even while living on this round ball of rock, it all seems small and inconsequential. I don't need to go to space for that." He paused. "I'm dyslexic, Dr. Swallows, and it doesn't just affect my reading and writing. Chaos is my enemy. Every loud noise or unwanted touch puts me on edge. So you can imagine how inviting being strapped inside a space vessel is to me."

That was a huge revelation. And one that needed to be addressed.

"I'm shocked you're even here," I told him. "I'd be happy to speak with Ms. Farnsworth on your behalf and explain the situation. You don't have to go on that flight tomorrow. In fact, you shouldn't."

All the astronauts needed to submit medical documentation before being allowed on the flight, and I wondered how his sensory issues had been overlooked.

He hesitated. "Unfortunately, I do."

"Noah, doing things that make you uncomfortable may be how you're used to living, but I don't feel it's wise for you to—"

He held up a hand. "Please don't tell anyone about this. I just... I needed to confide in someone. But I'm going to be on that flight tomorrow."

And then he stood, indicating that our time together was finished, regardless of what the clock said.

Noah turned back just before leaving. "Thank you for the past few days, Dr. Swallows. I needed it."

And then he walked out the door, and I didn't see him again until he'd donned his astronaut suit the next day and stood with the others outside the spacecraft.

They were going to space.

5

The launch wasn't nearly as exciting as one might think. All of us spaceport employees stood at a distance behind a barrier, everyone except Jeffrey, who was taking an official group photo of the seven astronauts. They all donned red suits and gloves and stood in front of the spacecraft, though it looked more like a wide airplane. The spacecraft was nestled between two wings, and once the plane reached a certain altitude, the spacecraft would disconnect, taking the astronauts the rest of the way.

Most of them had had no desire to talk to me the past few days, and I couldn't help but wonder what they'd think of this experience when they returned home. Would this be a life-changing event, as Julie had promised? Or would they be able to go back to their day-to-day lives and treat it as if they'd been on just another vacation—similar to Disneyland, or a day out on the yacht. Exciting while it lasted, but with no lingering effects once they were back in the real world.

Dr. Randall walked over to the astronauts and looked over the suits, checking that everything was how it should be. The suits had one pocket meant for a phone so the astronauts could take pictures. Charlotte had tried sneaking a box of cigarettes and a lighter in hers, and it was immediately confiscated.

"Mom, you could have gotten us all killed," Emma said, her lips pulled into a frown.

Once the seven astronauts boarded, the medical officer, Lori, followed. She would be the eighth passenger. Just in case.

And then, while the rest of us cheered and waved, the spacecraft started down the runway, no different than the way any other plane takes off for a flight.

Other than a final counseling session to unravel their space experience, my job was complete.

"We have two hours until they return," Jeffrey said, walking up to me as the employees returned inside. "Want to hit up the cafeteria? It just opened."

I glanced at my phone, not that I doubted him. Just wanted to see if we had time for both a first and second lunch before it closed again until dinner. Had to take advantage of all the amazing food, since it would all go away the next day. We'd been spoiled.

"Absolutely. I just need to run to the dorm to change into my stretchy pants." I was mostly kidding. As we reentered the building, I asked him, "What's it been like? Following the 'astronauts' around for the past few days?" I did air quotes around "astronauts." I knew it was marketed that way, but I didn't like that those bickering celebrities were now placed in a category with intelligent, brave men and women who had done so much good up there on the International Space Station, as well as those who had traveled farther.

I threw a backward glance toward the staff dorms when Jeffrey turned in the opposite direction down the hallway. I'd be okay without the stretchy pants. Probably.

"It was okay," he said with a small shrug. "I really like Ace Hutchins. He always seemed like a cool guy on TV, but he is that way in real life too. I was glad to not be disappointed. I like Rachel Sinclair too. Don't love her music—it's nothing special. But she wasn't in everybody's business, like the rest of them. Julie hoped the team-building exercises would help with cohesion, but it only seemed to make it worse."

I had missed a lot while stuck in my little office. There had been times I'd been able to sneak out and peek through windows, but most of the training exercises had been done behind closed doors, and I wasn't supposed to interrupt.

I thought of Rachel, who was used to stepping aside so she wasn't bowled over by the rest. After she'd left our one and only session, I'd wished she'd have returned so we could talk about some skills she could use to increase her self-confidence. Even famous singers had problems standing up for themselves, just like the rest of us.

"I take it that Charlotte was the center of the drama?"

Jeffrey opened the cafeteria door and motioned for me to enter.

"Forever and always," a man's voice said.

Dr. Randall appeared behind me, his gaze scanning the endless food choices. "That woman thrives on chaos, and she doesn't care what casualties are left in her wake. The problem is that the rest of the astronauts have a love/hate relationship with her. They need her, or at least they believe they do, but they despise her for it."

"Is it bad that I wish I hadn't missed all of it?" I asked, feeling sheepish. "It's like those daytime soap operas. You know they are ridiculous, but you also can't tear yourself away. And it was all happening in real time."

I decided on pizza for my first lunch, promising myself huevos rancheros for my second round.

"Count yourself lucky," Dr. Randall said. "I saw zero growth in any of them. I know they paid good money to be here, but honestly, I feel like this trip has been wasted on those seven."

"Even Serena?" I asked. "She came in to talk with me a couple of times, and even though I don't believe in all that psychic stuff, she seemed sweet."

"Sure. Until you tell her something she doesn't like. I saw the claws come out a few times with her. Never directed at me, but she wasn't about to let the others walk all over her. She placed herself in a dominant position and made sure the others respected that. I even saw her stand up to Charlotte a couple of times. Only one who did that."

Huh. And you think you know someone from a few therapy sessions.

Jeffrey had been right. Everything had been a show.

That was a bit disappointing, and it must have shown, because Dr. Randall nudged me with his shoulder. "Don't let it get you down. For what it's worth, I did think she was one of the more decent guests here. She was in survival mode, that's all."

I nodded. That made sense.

"That Noah guy, though," Jeffrey said, sliding onto the seat across from me at the table. "Didn't say a word the entire three days. Only watched and didn't participate

unless he was forced to. The others were rude, but at least they were making an effort. It was like he was too good for everyone there. I don't know why he even came."

Dr. Randall quietly ate his food, his gaze firmly focused on the enchilada in front of him.

He knew something. And I had a feeling it was more than just Noah's dyslexia.

"What do you think, Dr. Randall?" I asked.

He chewed his food far slower than necessary, then swallowed. "You're right. He doesn't want to be here." And then Dr. Randall stood. "You know, I think the launch took my appetite with it. I'll see you at the landing in..." He checked his watch. "Ninety minutes."

And then he dumped his tray and disappeared through a side door.

"That was weird, right?" Jeffrey asked, his gaze still on the door Dr. Randall had left through.

I agreed. "Very weird."

But that was nothing compared to when the spacecraft glided onto the runway ninety minutes later, the employees cheering. A small band played to the right of us, welcoming the astronauts home. Not sure where they came from.

That wasn't the weird part.

It was when six astronauts disembarked, instead of seven.

And then there was the scream.

6

L ori appeared in the entryway to the spacecraft. She held out her red-gloved hands, like it was supposed to mean something. Her expression was one of shock. Disbelief. Horror.

Portions of her gloves appeared to be darker than others.

Julie ducked under the barricade and hurried forward, as did Dr. Randall. They both spoke in hushed tones with the medical officer, then all three disappeared inside. When Julie reappeared, she was speaking on her cell phone. She abruptly ended the conversation, then immediately made another phone call, presumably to someone else.

The six astronauts stood to the side of the spacecraft as the band continued playing. They appeared confused about what was happening, as did the spectators. The engineers were concerned that they might have done something wrong and that the flight hadn't gone as expected. The two pilots had disembarked but seemed unsure if they were meant to leave or stay.

"What's going on?" Jeffrey whispered. "Which one is missing?"

Noah stood a short distance from the others, looking a bit worse for wear, which was understandable now that I knew how difficult that flight must have been for him. Rachel and Whitney stood in front of the craft, waving and smiling, bouncing to the beat of the band's music, seemingly unaware that anything unusual was happening. Serena stood at the back of the group, her gaze fixed firmly on the spacecraft, as if waiting for further instructions. The only ones who seemed to be in any kind of true distress were Ace and Emma, who kept throwing frantic looks back at the spacecraft. Emma folded her arms across her chest, like she was protecting herself from something.

"Charlotte," I said. "She didn't exit the spacecraft."

Jeffrey stood on his tiptoes, as if that would give him more of a clue as to what was going on. "Do you think she was injured?"

Could be. The way Julie and Dr. Randall were acting, though, it wasn't something benign like a sprained ankle. Something serious had occurred.

But if that was the case, why were the other astronauts acting like there was nothing wrong? It was as if they didn't notice Emma, who kept trying to go back on board. Officer Bridge was standing as sentry and wouldn't allow her past.

Her features held panic. Confusion. Her mother was no longer with the group, and no one would give her information, instead purposely keeping her away.

Jeffrey lifted his camera, but Julie spotted it from the spacecraft and made a quick, angry gesture for him to lower it.

They didn't want a record of whatever was happening right now.

The next order came from Officer Bridge. Everyone was to immediately return inside the spaceport, astronauts included, and we were to stay put for the time being. The cafeteria and recreational areas would remain open to all, but no one was to leave the building. For any reason.

As we filed in, I noticed the spaceport's firefighters and emergency response team rounding the corner of the building in their trucks, speeding faster than I thought safe with so many people still in the area. Officer Bridge collected cell phones from the medical officer and the six astronauts as they moved toward the spaceport, despite their many protests.

Something was seriously wrong here.

And all we were allowed to do was wait.

"I FEEL like I should be talking with the astronauts," I murmured to Jeffrey. We sat in a couple of high-backed chairs in one corner of the recreation hall. "Make sure they're doing all right. But it was made very clear to me that the only time I am allowed to speak with them is either in my office for a counseling session or if they are the ones to approach me."

Jeffrey wrung his hands, looking antsy. "Maybe if we go over to the arcades, we'll look more approachable." His voice shook slightly, and it gave me pause.

This whole time I'd been worried about the millionaire guests, but I hadn't even considered how everything—whatever that was, since we still hadn't been given any information—was affecting Jeffrey. I had never thought highly of the man, but really, he was still young. Still figuring life out.

"You doing okay?" I asked him, tilting my head to the side. He didn't look it. And it couldn't have been just the last hour that was weighing on his mind. Not with the dark circles under his eyes. I wondered if he'd gotten a decent night's sleep since arriving here three days earlier.

Jeffrey started to nod, but it then it morphed into a shake of the head. "No. This whole experience... It's been amazing. But I've also been stressed out of my mind. It's my first official photography job, at least my first job for someone that doesn't already know me. For someone who doesn't pity me. And the people I've been taking pictures of—they haven't wanted me here. I'm an intrusion. In their minds, I'm nothing more than sanctioned paparazzi."

"I'm so sorry. I wish I would have realized."

Moisture pooled in Jeffrey's eyes. "It's not your fault. I did my best to hide it. But I haven't been sleeping at night, Charlotte's voice berating me in my nightmares. She really is horrible. The worst. Maybe that's why no one is worried about something happening to her on the flight. Because no one cares."

And then the person I least expected to see at that moment walked into the room.

Sheriff Potts.

I stared.

I'd thought things were bad before. Now? I knew whatever had happened, it was disastrous.

Jeffrey was giving me a funny look, and I realized that he might have asked me a question. "What is so interesting that—" He turned in his seat. I knew the instant he'd spotted the sheriff. His gaze flew back to me so fast, it had to have made him dizzy. "What's Sheriff Potts doing here?" he whispered.

"That is a very good question." I had a feeling she was looking for someone.

The sheriff's gaze lingered on me for a moment before traveling to Emma Fischer. She quickly approached the woman and whispered in her ear, and then they left the room together.

I shifted my attention to the rest of the celebrities. Most had been gravitating to various activities, but as soon as Emma left, they made their way to the lounge chairs, somberness settling over the room, killing the desire to play the arcades or challenge anyone at the pool tables.

"What do you think that's about?" Rachel asked, her voice shaking. "It's Charlotte, isn't it? She didn't exit with the rest of us."

Ace Hutchins raised a shoulder. "I wouldn't be worried. She refused to unstrap her harness the entire time we were on the flight. I think she got a little more than she bargained for. Probably passed out on re-entry." His troubled eyes belied his words.

Whitney laughed. "The old woman got what she deserved."

"How can you say that at a time like this?" Rachel asked, flaring up. "The woman is a genius, and she deserves our sympathy."

"You're saying she ever agreed to make a dress for you?" Whitney threw a smirk in Rachel's direction.

She spluttered. "Well, n-no. But now that she's gotten to know me better, she might."

Emma re-entered the room, tear tracks on her cheeks. "No, she won't. Not now and not ever." She turned a hard stare on Rachel. "Last night I heard you approach her in the dorm. You asked for the millionth time. Begged her. She gave you another emphatic no and threatened to call security if you continued to harass her about it. Maybe you should focus more on your singing than the dress. Then you wouldn't have felt the need to kill her."

Rachel paled. "Killed her? Are you saying..."

Emma's eyes flashed. "Yes, my mother is dead. Murdered."

CHAOS ERUPTED. Rachel was angry that Emma had accused her of killing her mother, and Emma was angry at everyone in the room because one of them had to have done it. Noah looked bored, this new development not interesting him as much as I felt it should. Serena cowered at the edge of the group, eyeing everyone, as if they might jump from their chairs and attack her next. Whitney was telling Rachel she should have gone into acting instead of singing, since she cried on cue over Charlotte's death better than any of his previous costars. That left Ace attempting to calm everyone else down, to no avail.

Sheriff Potts put an end to that quickly when she speed-walked into the room and raised her fingers to her lips in the most ear-splitting whistle I'd ever heard.

"Stop it. All of you. I don't care who you are and if I'm supposed to recognize your name. I don't, by the way. Any of you. Because to me, you aren't celebrities. You aren't movie stars or famous singers. You are murder suspects. Seven of you went up in that spacecraft, and only six returned alive. I want to know why. If you lie to me, I will arrest you."

I had never been scared of our hometown sheriff. But in that moment, I was terrified. It seemed to have the same effect on the rest of the group, because it went deathly quiet. The celebrities didn't even dare glance at the others.

"Glad we have that cleared up," the sheriff said with a satisfied nod. "I'll be questioning each of you. Let's start with Dr. Swallows."

I was being questioned? I hadn't even been on board. "But—"

Sheriff Potts narrowed her eyes. "I am questioning everyone at the spaceport. Now move."

That was not a request.

I grabbed my purse, jumped from my chair, and followed the sheriff into the hallway.

As soon as the door shut behind us, the sheriff's whole countenance crumbled. "Sorry I barked at you like that. I couldn't show any weakness in front of those people. From what I understand, it fuels them, and I need to maintain the upper hand on this thing."

My pulse slowed. Good, I wasn't an actual suspect. I'd had enough of that in the past, and it hadn't exactly been my favorite pastime.

"I'm surprised to see you here," I said. "I thought Officer Bridge was in charge around here."

Sheriff Potts hesitated. "Yes, well, Officer Bridge is a glorified security guard, and there are some things he doesn't have authority to handle. Murder, for example." Even though her words were harsh, a softness had crossed her features at the mention of the security officer. When she noticed me watching her, she straightened and quickly changed the subject. "I'd heard through the grapevine that you and Lilly were hired part-time, and I have to say, I'm glad you're here. I could use your help."

Danielle Potts needed my help. Now I knew things were bad.

"Where's Lilly?" she asked, glancing around, as if my daughter would materialize at my side.

Guess the grapevine hadn't gotten all the facts.

"Back in Amor, sick. I talked with her yesterday. She's feeling a lot better but devastated at not being here. This... situation...should help her not feel so bad about missing out."

The sheriff smirked. "Knowing your kids, she'd rather be here. But I, for one, am grateful she's at home. I don't need another fiasco like at the hot air balloon festival."

I tried to trap a laugh, but it escaped as a snort. It was true that my kids liked to poke their noses where they weren't allowed and get into the middle of things they shouldn't. Lilly and her brother had crawled around a murder scene at the festival and eaten the dead man's snacks, after all.

"Who's the wiry kid you were sitting with?" the sheriff asked, nodding to the closed door.

"Jeffrey Monroe. You know, Karen's kid."

The sheriff's lips parted. "The photographer who ruined that wedding last summer?"

"Yup."

She groaned. "I was fielding complaints for a month because of that guy. And the spaceport hired him?"

I lifted a shoulder. "They were desperate."

"No kidding."

A pause.

"You're sure Charlotte was murdered, then?" I asked.

Sheriff Potts' gaze swept the hallway, and then she ensured the recreation room doors were fully closed. "Yes. I don't need to tell you how bad this looks for the spaceport. Two decades' worth of progress could disappear overnight if this gets out. And if the spaceport disappears, so does a good portion of Amor's economy. Ever since its inaugural flight, deals have been made to revitalize the town. Space tourism brings in big money from all over the world. In short..."

"This could be devastating to more than just the billionaire, Ted Carson, and his space tourism company." The gravity of the situation settled over me. "You think people aren't going to find out that an international fashion icon is dead?" I blew out a hard breath. "They're going to know before the end of the day."

Sheriff Potts' gaze hardened. "Not if I can help it. Not before I have found my murderer."

7

The adrenaline of the past hour hadn't allowed the gravity of the situation to fully sink in.

There was a murderer among us.

"How was she killed?" I asked, pacing the hallway. Nervous energy pulsed through me, and I didn't know what to do with it. "I mean, they were in an enclosed space."

Sheriff Potts motioned for me to follow her down the hallway. "Let's talk in your office. I was told I could use it for questioning. I hope you don't mind. Julie thought it might help put the astronauts more at ease."

"She's worried about the impact this will have on their flight experience, and in turn, future flights," I said, immediately seeing it from a PR point of view. Even with someone being murdered on board, they were trying to make the best of the situation. And if the astronauts returned home and said they were treated with utmost respect during the entire ordeal, maybe the spaceport's reputation could still be salvaged.

Good thing Julie hadn't been there for the sheriff's threats.

"I understand her perspective," the sheriff said, ushering me into my office and closing the door. "But their feelings don't matter much to me at the moment. And the reputation of the spaceport won't matter much if I don't find the killer."

I placed my purse on a side table and then sat on the couch usually reserved for the astronauts. "How was she murdered?" I asked, repeating the question from earlier.

Sheriff Potts leaned against the door. "She was stabbed and was left to bleed to death."

I stared. "You're telling me that the woman was stabbed by a knife on a small spacecraft, with seven other people there, and no one noticed a thing? Aren't there cameras on board? Surely someone must have seen something."

"The video feed from the spacecraft is being retrieved even as we speak. Because you're right, someone had to have seen it happen. And if they did, why are they keeping quiet about it? While we wait, we're taking care of the body and will allow Emma to say goodbye. Dr. Harris will transport it back to Amor. He's on his way now."

I snorted. Not because the situation was funny in the slightest, but because of the thought of our town doctor-slash-mortician, Dr. Harris, preparing the body of a famous fashion designer. The man was very good at what he did, but he had a folksy charm that I doubted Charlotte would have approved of.

My smile dipped when the sheriff gave me a side glance and her mouth tightened into a stern line.

"Sheriff, how can I be of help?"

She was quiet for a moment, almost like she was trying to choose her words carefully, or maybe she was afraid she was making a mistake by including me in the investigation. There had been times in the past when we'd worked together, but it had usually been because I'd forced myself into it.

"This situation is delicate," Sheriff Potts said. "Officer Bridge has already confiscated the phones of everyone on board, and I'm hoping we'll find clues that might help us figure out what happened. They were allowed to take photos during the four minutes they experienced zero gravity."

"Microgravity," I said, the response coming automatically. I'd researched it when I'd first learned I'd be working at the spaceport.

The technicalities didn't matter, and I wished I'd kept it to myself when the sheriff threw me an annoyed glance. "What?"

"Microgravity. The spacecraft is essentially moving so fast that the astronauts are constantly falling, making it seem like there is no gravity. Same as on the International

Space Station. The space station orbits the Earth every one and a half hours, if you can believe it—"

The sheriff gave me a look that made my lips clamp shut.

"Microgravity," I whispered, then cleared my throat. "Anyway, taking away their cell phones is smart, and not just because you need clues. You don't want them calling anyone, telling them what's going on, before you have a handle on things."

Sheriff Potts looked like she might be annoyed with me, but then her features relaxed and she shrugged. "Yes, that too. I'm not blind. I know it's wishful thinking that no one will leak the story to the press. But the longer we can go without the media involved, the better. Now that their phones are with me, I can begin questioning everyone."

"You still haven't said what you want me to do." Sheriff Potts hadn't invited me for a private chat because she'd missed me.

The sheriff's gaze settled on me. "I want you to be my eyes and ears. Sit in the room with the others. Listen. Be as invisible as possible. Someone is bound to slip up."

"They know I work here. I've had them all in my office," I said. "Won't they assume I'll report anything that seems unusual?"

"Nope."

Sheriff Potts didn't tell me exactly how she planned on making that happen, but after she handed me my purse, escorted me back to the rec room and threw open the door, I began to understand.

"Don't think I'm done with you yet," she said to me in a commanding voice. "Particularly because I didn't like your answers."

Guess I wasn't being given the choice if I wanted to be a spy or not. And not only was she going to treat me the same as the others, something told me she was going to treat me worse.

Sheriff Potts glanced at a piece of paper in her hand, like she was following some sort of order she'd been given from a higher-up. "Emma Fischer, can I see you for a moment?"

Emma stood, her legs shaking. "I'm not sure I'm up to answering any questions at the moment, ma'am." I suddenly felt sorry for her. No matter the lifestyle she was used to living, or how poorly Charlotte had treated people, Emma had just lost her mother, and that would be hard on anyone.

The sheriff's tone softened. "It's not about that." She then nodded toward the door.

"All right." Emma threw the room a departing glance and left with the sheriff.

The other astronauts were not as kind as Sheriff Potts had been, and she had been absolutely right when she'd said the others would talk around me.

"I'll bet a million dollars that she's the one who killed

Charlotte," Whitney said. "She was sitting right across the aisle from her, wasn't she?"

"Why would she do that?" Ace asked his friend, his nose scrunched up in confusion. "They seemed like two peas in a pod."

Whitney laughed. "Two peas is right. They were both vindictive and too caught up in their own success to care about anyone else. And since Emma has been living off her mother's fame and fortune all these years..." He raised an eyebrow, like we should fill in the blank.

"Emma is an artist," Serena said. "She's supposed to be a little reclusive." She'd moved in closer, seemingly trying to be more a part of things now that Charlotte was gone and couldn't punish her for her prediction. The one that had proved to be true.

"Sure, if painting canvases in your mom's attic counts as being an artist," Rachel said. "Despite her claims, the woman has never sold a single piece of artwork, instead using it as an excuse to live off her mom while she was 'building a following.'" She used air quotes around the last part. "Now that her mom's dead, she doesn't have to pretend anymore. Can be herself for the first time, ever. I tell you what, if I were Emma, I'd have killed my mom too."

Silence settled over the group, and they were no doubt wondering the same thing I was. If Rachel would kill her own mother for money, was it possible that she could kill someone else as well? Maybe someone she resented for not designing a gown for her. Something that was rumored to be essential to win Rachel's long sought-after Grammy.

Noah sat at the snack bar that ran along the back of the lounge area and snorted. It was the first indication that he'd even been listening to the conversation.

Whitney threw a glance toward him. "You have something to add to the conversation?"

Noah stayed quiet. Didn't even look at Whitney.

That seemed to make the actor more upset than if Noah had responded.

Whitney stood from his seat and made to move toward Noah, but Ace jumped in between them. "Leave him alone, Whit."

"Why? For all we know, he's the one who offed the lady. It's not like we know anything about him. And it's not like he's been making an effort to rectify that. Whatever we do, he's too good for us. We were told we needed to have each other's backs up there in space. But did he have anyone's back? Not in the slightest. Unless sticking a knife in Charlotte's is how he interpreted the assignment."

"Like you have had anyone's back," Emma said, entering the room. "Including your so-called best friend." Even though her eyes were filled with moisture, her back was straight and she held her head high. Sheriff Potts was right. Weakness was not allowed with this group, and Emma knew it. Now that her mom—her protection—was gone, she'd need to fend for herself.

Whitney spun toward Emma. "What is that supposed to mean?"

Emma rolled her eyes. "We all know that you resent Ace for being more successful than you are. You both went to the same acting school, and yet he's an A-list actor, and, unlike my mom, I wouldn't even consider you B-list. You're the guy who sometimes gets a good part but most of the time ends up as a recurring character on a sitcom no one has ever heard of. You ride on Ace's coattails."

When Whitney opened his mouth to protest, she waved a hand to stop him. "Don't bother pretending."

Whitney's hands balled into fists, and he looked like he'd have no problem hitting a woman who'd just lost her mother. Of course, Emma wasn't exactly acting like a grieving daughter.

"That's not true, is it?" Ace asked, turning to his friend. His eyes held genuine concern. Like he'd considered Whitney his closest friend and was now being told otherwise.

"Of course it's true," Whitney snapped. "I've worked ten times harder than you—and I'm ten times more talented as well. But you skate through life, never having to worry about if you'll get the part, or if you can afford another house in Italy or Paris, or wherever it is you're buying houses nowadays."

Ace opened his mouth, then closed it, momentarily at a loss for words. "But I always invite you to the parties and the auditions and—"

"And I'm tired of being your sidekick," Whitney said.

"Is that why you killed Charlotte?" Rachel mused from her seat. "Because you were angry with her for calling you out the other day? Seems silly, really, because it wouldn't have accomplished anything. But, of course, murder is rarely rational."

Whitney turned on her. "You would know, wouldn't you?"

She scoffed. "You think I killed her? Just because I hated the woman didn't mean I had any desire to kill her." She paused. "That's not true. I did have the desire. Lucky for me, someone else beat me to it."

I turned to where Jeffrey had sat, hardly believing this conversation was even taking place.

But he wasn't there.

His camera sat on the floor by the vacated chair, but he was nowhere to be seen.

"Did anyone see where Jeffrey went off to?" I asked before thinking better of it.

Every head swiveled toward me. Shoot, I was supposed to be invisible.

"Who?" Rachel asked.

I raised an eyebrow. "Jeffrey. The photographer who has been following you around for the past three days?"

Everyone's eyes lit up in recognition.

"Oh, the goofy-looking fellow," Whitney said. "Yeah, a little while after the sheriff pulled you out for your interrogation, he ran from the room. Looked like he was about to pee his pants."

Upon further investigation, I learned that not only had Jeffrey run from the room, he'd run from the building. Security had been busy elsewhere and hadn't been able to stop him.

"Lilly never would have run," I muttered, annoyed. Turned out that Sheriff Potts didn't care. She was glad to be rid of him.

She smiled and said, "Good. Now the real investigation can begin."

8

"He was only going to get in the way," Sheriff Potts said, leaning against my desk. "And he was considerate enough to leave his camera for you to look through, so now we don't need him."

I had been pulling a sip from my water bottle and choked. "You want me to look through his camera?"

"I'm busy with interrogations. Every employee and guest in the building has to be questioned. You have something else you'd rather be doing?"

Many things. But all of them required me being able to leave the spaceport.

So, I returned to the rec room, where things had calmed down a bit. Whitney and Rachel were playing pool. Serena and Emma were speaking in hushed tones in the lounge area, while Ace played at one of the arcades.

Noah was the only one missing. I didn't ask anyone where he'd gone, because he wouldn't have told them.

I'd just settled into a chair in the corner of the room, Jeffrey's camera in my hands, when my phone burst into song. I scrambled to silence it, but with the camera in one hand while I tried to pull the phone out of my purse, I was all thumbs. Benji's picture filled the screen, and I desperately wished I could answer it and tell him everything that was going on. His presence, or even his voice, would be such a comfort right now.

After managing to silence the phone's ringtone, I pretended I hadn't noticed anything unusual, but every head in the room had turned toward me.

"You have a phone," Emma said, her gaze fixed on me.

I opened my mouth, ready to refute her claim, but it would be an obvious lie, and as a psychologist, I was meant to be a trusted confidante.

"Yes," I said. "I wasn't on the flight, so I wasn't required to turn it in." I gave her a smile, like my hands weren't sweating so much that I was resisting the urge to wipe them on my pants. "Thank goodness, because I need to check in with my kids, who are at home. They worry."

Emma took a step toward me, and Rachel stood, following suit. "I need to use your phone," Emma said.

"As do I," Whitney said.

Rachel turned on him. "Me first."

Even Serena wasn't immune to the lure of technology, her gaze eager. "I don't want my son to worry, either," she said with a smile. I'd thought of us as something akin to friends, or at least the closest thing that anyone in this group could come to it, but she was currently eyeing me like she was the cheetah and I was the gazelle in one of those nature documentaries. And I was fairly certain she didn't even have a son.

The rec room door opened. "Not taking your phone was an oversight on my part." Sheriff Potts strode up to me, slightly out of breath, and extended a hand. "Phone. Now."

I glanced up at the ceiling, looking for security cameras, but didn't see any. How had the sheriff known what had been happening? There was no way her timing was that good.

I handed my phone over, but not without some grumbling to let her know I wasn't happy about it. "I wasn't anywhere near the spacecraft."

"Would you rather spend the afternoon in interrogation? Because I can arrange that."

Noah walked in at that moment, a burrito in hand. "It would be better than being trapped in this place. There's fewer crazy people in an insane asylum."

So, the man had decided to speak. And the first thing he'd done was insult everyone. I squeezed my eyes shut, desperately wishing this was a nightmare. That would mean I could wake up. But I didn't wake, and when I opened my eyes, it was to five glaring faces, all looking murderously toward Noah. True to form, he didn't look like he could care less.

But chances were one of those that he had just insulted was a murderer.

Sheriff Potts straightened. "It's your lucky day, Dr. Swallows. Rather than you coming to my office, Noah and I—we're going to have a bit of a chat." She looked at him and pointed toward the door.

I was left staring long after they were gone.

Whitney whistled. "That sheriff doesn't mess around, does she? You think she really believes Noah did it?"

"Wouldn't be the first time she'd accused someone wrongly of murder," I said. Because there was no way Noah had done it. He had no motive. And he certainly didn't have the personality for it.

That got everyone's attention.

"So..." Serena started, like she was trying to figure out how to put her thoughts into words. "You know the sheriff well, then?"

That was a complicated question.

"Sort of." And now I saw this for what it was. Sheriff Potts had thrown me into the inner circle. I was now one of them. My phone had been taken away, like them. I'd been yelled at—threatened. Like them.

I made my way toward the lounge area and flopped into one of the chairs. "I'm just tired of everything, you know? I want to go home to my kids. Heck, I'm even missing my mother, which I never thought I'd say. But now Sheriff Potts has us all trapped in this place. Is it my fault that I tend to be in the wrong place at the wrong time? I swear, things like this follow me around."

I realized I'd laid it on a bit thick and wished I could backpedal, especially considering that I was surrounded by professional actors. And even those who didn't do it as a career had long ago learned the art of acting as a means of survival.

They didn't seem to notice my terrible acting skills, however, and moved in, intrigued. Even Serena was on the edge of her seat. "You mean, you've been a murder suspect before?"

I nodded.

Rachel inched closer. "What's it like?" If I didn't know any better, I'd have sworn her intrigue had morphed into something else.

Excitement.

I blew out a hard breath. "It's stressful, of course. A lot of questions. That woman knows how to wear you down."

Serena turned slightly in her seat, throwing a glance at me. I could have been mistaken, but I'd have sworn she looked...disappointed.

"What is it?"

Her eyes narrowed slightly. "A psychologist who has a history of being a murder suspect, and you were hired on by Galactic Enterprises? Doubtful."

"I've never actually murdered anyone, of course. I don't have a criminal record or anything like that."

Serena nodded but didn't say anything more. She

worried me. Not because I believed she really was a psychic, but because in her line of work, she had to have honed incredible observational skills. And even though I didn't believe she was the real deal, others might. And they could be swayed. Because she was one of them. And as much as I pretended, I was not.

I needed to become friends with these celebrities; that was how the sheriff was going to find a murderer.

Or maybe she already had.

For all I knew, Noah was the killer, with his detached ways. Sure, many murderers have been people pleasers— the friendly neighbor that no one would ever suspect. The one who gained your trust. But many others had been the one on the outside of society. The quiet one who kept to themselves. The one you never gave a second glance, until they forced you to.

I'd learned that from my ex-husband. Sometimes his disturbing specialization at the university, the psychology of serial killers, came in handy. The kids and I had become desensitized to his gruesome stories long ago.

Sheriff Potts showed up in the doorway several minutes later, her gaze scanning the gathered group. Noah squeezed in around her, nearly done with his burrito. I wondered if the sheriff had managed to get anything out of him or if he'd merely eaten his way through the interrogation as he'd done in our therapy sessions.

"Serena, I need to see you in my office, please," Sheriff Potts said, her gaze having found its target.

Wow, the celebrity psychic had elicited politeness from the sheriff. Serena looked pleased and followed the sheriff from the room, but I saw it for what it was.

Serena was in trouble.

What motive would Serena have for killing the fashion icon, though?

It was halfway through dinner when I found out.

I wished the sheriff could have waited an hour, because the moment the sheriff pulled me into my office, I lost my appetite.

And the chicken cordon bleu had looked so good too. I hoped there would be some left when I returned.

9

"Looks like I don't need your help after all," Sheriff Potts said, leaning against my desk. "You can retrieve your things and head home."

I shouldn't have asked questions. All I needed to do was say "okay," grab my suitcase, and run.

But I didn't. Because it made no sense. Unless the sheriff had found damning evidence in the footage from the spacecraft, there wasn't enough information to go on.

I cocked an eyebrow. "You haven't even questioned everyone yet."

"Don't need to. Everything points back to one person. Serena Barre."

Now, that definitely didn't seem right. "Did she confess?"

"That's not something murderers are inclined to do," Sheriff Potts said. "At least not the ones I've come across."

Even though she sounded confident, her expression held doubt.

"Mind sharing with me why your sights have settled on her? Because from where I'm standing, no one should be ruled out. Serena didn't run in the same circles as Charlotte. Why would she want her dead?"

Sheriff Potts lifted a finger. "You'd think they hadn't met before this little trip, wouldn't you? Turns out that Serena spent quite a lot of time with Charlotte. The fashion icon drove Serena out to her house as much as three times a week to do readings. It wasn't Charlotte who chose who to make dresses for. It was Serena. She would read the energy of those requesting custom dresses, and then would choose the ones that vibrated in the right way, or something like that. I don't understand all that other-worldly kind of stuff."

I ran my fingers through my hair. When Charlotte had called Serena a quack, she had done it as if she didn't believe in psychics. And all along, it had just been another show. One meant to cover up the fact that not only did she believe in psychics, but her whole business revolved around one.

"So what, Serena helped Charlotte choose which clients to work with. It doesn't explain why Serena would want her dead."

"No, it doesn't," the sheriff said. "But she did predict Charlotte's death, didn't she? Right before Charlotte insulted her in front of everyone. I heard that you were there."

I flashed back to when I'd stood outside the room with the centrifuge. Serena had told Charlotte that she and her work would be missed.

That did look pretty bad. I wondered how the sheriff had found out about that. Probably Lori, the medical officer.

"It doesn't prove anything," I said, collapsing onto the couch.

Sheriff Potts repositioned my office chair and sat in it so that she was facing me. "We found the murder weapon. It was tucked into one of the straps under Serena's seat on the spacecraft. The way we figure it, Serena stabbed Charlotte while Charlotte was seated. She was stabbed in the side that was facing the spacecraft, so no one noticed the wound, and Serena was able to quickly hide the knife under her seat before anyone saw."

I frowned. Yes, that looked bad for Serena. But I didn't think it was enough to arrest her over. Not yet, anyway. "Is someone putting pressure on you to finish this thing up quickly?" I asked. "Because you are a good sheriff, and you're always thorough. It feels like you're rushing things, though, and it's not good police work."

I expected the sheriff to be angry with me—I tended to bring that side out of her—but she didn't say anything. Just sat there, watching me.

So, I continued.

"First off, she has no motive. Second, why would Serena stash the murder weapon under her own seat, when she had to have known you'd find it there? The killer would place it under someone else's seat, right? And this isn't a carriage ride through a park. I saw Emma right after experiencing the centrifuge. It's an intense journey where they are trying their best to not pass out from the pressure they are experiencing. The murder would have had to take place during the four minutes of microgravity. Have you asked anyone if they talked to Charlotte during those four minutes? Do you even have a time of death? You said you'd been looking at the footage from the flight. Did anyone come close enough to her to kill her? How did the knife get on the spacecraft in the first place? I saw Dr. Randall checking to make sure no one tried sneaking contraband onto the flight. A necessary protocol ever since the inaugural flight when that old lady managed to take knitting needles on board. Talk about a safety concern."

Sheriff Potts stood from the chair so fast that it crashed behind her. She didn't seem angry, though. Instead, her eyes held a deep frustration I'd never seen. She held her hands up. "You're right. But if our celebrity astronauts aren't on their scheduled flights home tomorrow, this entire thing blows up. Everyone will be under scrutiny. The spaceport. The astronauts. I'm receiving calls every five minutes from Ted Carson himself, asking about my progress, and I've only just begun the investigation."

I understood where the sheriff was coming from. I did.

But that wasn't any excuse for all these unanswered questions.

"And if you arrest the wrong person?" I asked.

Sheriff Potts nodded. "I know. There's no excuse for rushing through this case." She released a hard breath, then straightened. "We're going to do this the right way. No shortcuts. And Mr. Carson is just going to have to deal with it."

"Let's start with fingerprints," I said. "Any on the knife?"

The sheriff gave a humorless laugh. "They were all wearing gloves for the flight. No fingerprints. And whoever our culprit is must have touched everything in that spacecraft because there were traces of blood on every seatbelt, on every seat....everywhere. It wasn't visible to the naked eye, but it was there. The killer knew exactly what they were doing."

Right.

"What about the video you pulled from the flight?"

"Don't have anything useful from that, either. Charlotte Fischer isn't visible at all, because everyone else is flying around, blocking our view. According to Emma, Charlotte had no desire to tumble around the spacecraft like a common clown. She preferred to take in the view, so she remained restrained for the entire trip."

I was beginning to see why the sheriff had been getting desperate for anything she could cling on to. Seven astronauts had gone up, six had returned alive. No fingerprints. No eyewitnesses.

"Why didn't the medical officer notice anything?" I asked. "Surely Lori would have noticed someone bleeding out. She does check everyone's restraints, doesn't she?"

"Apparently, when you don't have gravity, blood acts differently. It can splatter further than normal, unconstrained by gravity. Or it can just kind of pool into a dome around a wound, making it difficult to even see where the wound is. Charlotte was the latter. And their suits were red, making it even worse."

"So, when did she actually die, then?" If she hadn't bled out during those four minutes then—"No one noticed anything because she didn't die until re-entry. When they now had gravity and all that pressure pushing down on their chests." My hand flew to my mouth. I thought I'd be sick. "How did no one notice when they disembarked?" I whispered.

"Most of the blood soaked her spacesuit and the seat." Sheriff Potts tried to sound matter-of-fact, but her face had gone ashen. "There was some on the floor, of course. But no one had to move around her to exit the spacecraft. There was a lot going on, and everyone was focused on their own thing."

I squeezed my eyes shut. This murder investigation was far from over. When I opened them, I saw that the sheriff was watching me with concern. "Why didn't she say anything when she'd been stabbed? Make a noise? Something to alert the others?"

Sheriff Potts raised a shoulder. She was at as much of a loss as I was.

"If I were you, I'd interrogate everyone a second time. A third time, even. Someone had to have seen what happened," I said.

The sheriff released a long breath. "You're likely right. In the meantime, though, I do need to detain Serena. There is enough circumstantial evidence that I don't feel comfortable allowing her to have full access to the facility and everyone in it. Not until I have more to go on."

It made sense, and I couldn't fault her for her caution. "You got to do what you got to do. But Sheriff?" I held out a hand. "I want my phone back."

She hesitated, likely thinking back to the hunger the celebrities had shown when they'd realized I had a way to contact the outside world.

"I promise I'll put it on vibrate."

The sheriff gave in and pulled my phone out of the desk drawer and handed it over. "Text me if you discover anything that might be useful."

"Will do." I paused. "How did you know what was going on—that the others had discovered my phone?"

Sheriff Potts's lips tugged up at one corner. "I'm good at what I do." And then she looked pointedly at the door. That was my cue to leave.

I left the office, not pushing the issue. For now. I was

more anxious to finally sit down with Jeffrey's camera and sift through the pictures. He had to have captured something that would be helpful.

The celebrities were still lounging in the rec room when I returned, complaining that there wasn't anything to do, so I relocated to the cafeteria. If I was going to be working, I might as well eat while doing it. That and I didn't want prying eyes looking over my shoulder, wondering what I was up to.

It was from Jeffrey's pictures that I caught my first glimpse of the centrifuge. It was massive. The circular room that housed it was bare, shining red tile gleaming on the walls. And in the middle...something that looked like it could belong in an amusement park. The contraption had two long metal arms that spanned the room and pivoted around a metal cylinder that was bolted to the floor. On the end of one of the arms was a capsule that looked kind of like the cockpit of a fighter jet.

"Intimidating, isn't it?" Dr. Randall had sneaked up behind me at some point, startling me.

"You actually strapped them into that thing?"

Dr. Randall nodded. "They needed to learn how to breathe with six times their weight pressing in on them." He grabbed a napkin and drew a stick person on it for me. "There are two types of g-force, one that presses down on you, and one that presses against you. When the pressure is coming down on you," he drew arrows pointing down, "it forces the blood from your head and into your legs."

"Which would make you pass out," I said.

"Exactly. When it presses against you, it makes it hard to breathe. The pressure doesn't last the entire flight, but when it does, the astronauts need to be prepared so they can be conscious for their one shot at going to space."

That sounded terrifying, and it made me grateful I was on the administrative side of the spaceport.

"Anyone pass out in training?" I asked.

Dr. Randall's eyes lit up, and he leaned in close. "Every one of them. Well, except Serena. They just couldn't concentrate—or wouldn't. I've been uncomfortable with the dynamics of this group since the very beginning, and it showed in their training. None of them were prepared."

"Did any of that have to do with Charlotte?"

Dr. Randall leaned back. "If she was having a bad day, everyone was having a bad day. Charlotte was the popular one of the group, but not the good kind. She was the one that everyone craved attention from, and yet they simultaneously resented her for it."

"Except Emma, of course," I said as I scrolled. Looked like they had had a group volleyball game. Except, in addition to Noah, it seemed Charlotte had refused to participate in this activity. They both sat along the sidelines. Julie had joined a team to even things out. In a few of the pictures, Ace and Whitney looked to be playing one-handed.

"Oh, no, even Emma couldn't handle her mother," Dr. Randall said. "The way she would glare at her mother when she wasn't looking—well, Emma's probably the reason behind the cliché *If looks could kill*."

But that didn't mean she had killed Charlotte. Of course, if Emma stood to inherit everything her mother had built, that could be motive.

I tilted the camera's screen toward Dr. Randall. "Why are Ace and Whitney playing with one hand behind their backs?"

He laughed when he saw the picture. "It was an exercise to help them be more aware of their space, no pun intended. Because of how reactive everything is in microgravity to movement, accidentally bumping someone could send them hurtling into the side of the spacecraft. To help prevent injury, there are no sharp edges on board, but Julie wanted to help the astronauts be more aware of their surroundings as well as work on their teamwork."

"Looks like not everyone was a team player." I tossed a glance at the camera. "Including the ones who are actually playing."

Dr. Randall's smile disappeared. "When you watch the video feed from their four minutes of microgravity, they were bouncing all over and crashing into each other. It was like they hadn't listened to a word we'd said. I'm surprised there was only one dead body when they returned."

That seemed a bit harsh, but I could understand the sentiment.

My phone began to vibrate in my pocket. I didn't answer it at first, forgetting that the celebrities weren't in the room with me. When it continued, I pulled it from my pocket and saw it was Flash calling.

"I'm sorry, it's my son," I said, holding up the phone. "I need to answer this."

Dr. Randall waved me on. "Of course. I need to get back to work, anyway. Just because there was a murder doesn't mean the world's stopped turning."

So true, and yet it felt wrong to admit it. Because somebody's world had stopped turning. Just not his.

"Hey, hon," I said when I finally managed to answer the phone. "Everything okay at home?"

Heavy breathing.

"Flash?" Even though I had no reason to believe that something was wrong, or that he was in danger, my pulse quickened.

"Mom, you have to listen to me very carefully." His voice was barely a whisper, like he didn't want to be overheard. "First, I've been able to look up some information you're going to want in regard to your murder victim."

Before I could ask how he could possibly know anything about that, he continued. "Second, Grandma's on her way to break into the spaceport. And she's dragged me and Lilly along for the ride."

10

M y mind went blank. Any ability I'd had to think
clearly had vanished with my son's words.

"You there, Mom?"

I shook myself, forcing myself to focus. "Yeah, sorry.
But you did not just tell me that your grandma is planning
on breaking into the spaceport. That would be crazy."

And just the kind of thing she would do if she thought
I was involved in another murder investigation. We'd been
estranged for so many years, she was trying to make up for
lost time. Trying to protect her only child. At least that was
what I told myself. It was better than admitting that my
mother was insane. Especially if it turned out that it was
genetic.

"We'll be there in thirty minutes," Flash said.

I sucked in a long breath, forcing myself to be calm.

This was fine. It was okay. I'd just need to warn Julie and Officer Bridge. They'd take care of it.

"How did you even find out about the murder?" I asked.

"Jeffrey Monroe. He called his mom on his way back to town, and the whole town knew about what happened before he'd even arrived." There was a pause and then some background whispering. "Lilly wants you to know that she's furious she was replaced with an incompetent photographer like him. And she's annoyed that you got to meet Ace Hutchins. And Rachel...something. I can't tell what she's saying. But she's wondering if Grandma pulls this off if it would be too much for her to ask for an autograph or two. You know, considering the situation."

Of course she was.

"You can tell her that no, she can't have an autograph and that she has no reason to be upset with me for leaving her behind. I wasn't the one who ate day-old lasagna that had been left out on the counter. She probably had food poisoning."

A pause.

"Yeah, that wasn't day-old lasagna. It had been out for closer to four days."

Oh. I could already hear my mother's voice in the back of my head. The one that said if I was home more, I would have known that. But it was difficult being a single mom, a business owner, and a contributing member of the community. And oh yeah, I had a boyfriend now. It was still weird to admit that.

There were so many demands pulling at me all the time, I couldn't keep track of every little detail. Like how long a plate of lasagna had been sitting in the kitchen.

"Flash, I can't thank you enough for calling. The folks here wouldn't take kindly to you randomly showing up on a good day, let alone with everything that's going on right now. I'll try to take care of things on my end, but in the meantime, see if you can convince your grandma to turn around and go home, would you?"

My mom's voice suddenly filled the line. She must have caught the kids on the phone and had Flash put the call on speaker.

"Maddie, I can't believe you're involved with another murder. Not only is that irresponsible, but you didn't call me. You know I feel left out when you go out on your adventures and I'm the only one left in the dark."

I released an exasperated sigh. My mom wasn't concerned that I'd been present for yet another murder. She was annoyed that I hadn't called to tell her about it.

"I didn't call Trish, either," I said. "Speaking of which, does she know that you kidnapped the children?"

"Oh, no, she had to go back to the office and asked if I would stay and keep an eye on things for the afternoon."

That didn't sound like Trish. She knew Flash was old enough to be alone for a few hours.

My mom, however, was convinced that even I needed constant supervision.

"You invited yourself over, didn't you?"

She chuckled. "Of course not. In any case, I left a note letting her know where the kids and I had run off to."

My heart stalled. "But Mom—"

"We're coming to the spaceport to help get you out of this mess, and that's final. You don't think I'd let you put yourself in harm's way and offer no support, do you? That's what families do."

"But—"

The line went dead.

I stared at the silent phone in my hand.

If Trish was home from work, she'd absolutely be freaking out by now.

I sent her a quick text as I hurried toward the administrative offices.

I needed to warn Julie.

IF SOMETHING WAS GOING to be the straw that broke the camel's back, this was it. Julie's usually calm and businesslike manner had been reduced to that of someone who was on the verge of an emotional breakdown. She paced the small area of her office, empty trays from the cafeteria littered around the desk, her eyes red and puffy as if she'd been crying. I wondered if it would help for her to step into my office for an hour.

"This isn't a hotel," she said.

"Trust me, I don't like it any more than you do," I told her. "But as soon as my mom caught wind that there had been a murder, well, she worried. And I have no problem with you turning her away at the security booth. In fact, I'd prefer it. But I must warn you that she's a force of nature, and she doesn't let much stop her."

Julie's gaze snapped up, and she looked like she was having trouble breathing. "How did she hear about the murder?"

"Jeffrey Monroe."

She slumped into a nearby chair. "So much for him signing an NDA. We can sue him, you know. But I doubt he has more than a couple of dollars to his name." She lifted her hands in a helpless gesture. "This is it. The end of the road for me. Even if Galactic Enterprises is able to continue after this, I'm done for. I'll never work again."

I pulled up a chair, sat across from her, and began to take full, deep breaths. I'd been laughed at before, because no one believed that deep breaths did anything other than make a person look stupid. It was too simple to be useful. But when people panicked, they tended to take shallow breaths. This meant less oxygen for their brain, which meant impaired decision-making. Science backed it up, but people liked to think of it as some New Age thing.

Not Julie, though.

She mimicked me and took a long, deep breath. I'd

thought she might have done it subconsciously, but then she gave me a slight smile.

"Thank you," she said.

I returned the smile, but it didn't last long. "I'm sorry that my family is the source of additional stress. I tried calling my mom back to tell her to abort the plan, but she didn't answer. She knows when she's doing something she shouldn't, and she puts on this elderly lady persona, like she didn't know better. Old people always know better, they've just figured out how to use their age to their advantage."

Julie laughed. "She sounds like a character. And under different circumstances, I'm sure I'd have loved to meet her." She massaged her forehead. "But now is not a good time, no matter her intentions."

"I couldn't agree more. Just wanted to give you fair warning in case she makes it as far as the front desk."

Julie stood, her breathing now steady. "I appreciate the concern, but our security here is top notch. You recall how much paperwork you needed just to walk onto the premises. They would never let an elderly woman and her grandchildren just walk into the spaceport. You focus on making sure our astronauts aren't emotionally scarred from this experience, and we'll send your family home with free T-shirts or something so they won't feel like the drive out here was a total waste."

"Thank you for understanding."

That was one problem taken care of. Now for the other part of my job: make sure a group of celebrities weren't emotionally scarred when one of them could be a murderer. And figure out which one it was.

11

I had just left Julie's office when my phone vibrated with a new text. It was from the sheriff.

Anything useful on the camera?

I paused in the hallway and typed a quick *No. I'll keep trying.*

My phone vibrated again after I'd managed only a couple more steps.

Just finished interviewing Rachel. I need you back where the others are. Remember: my eyes and ears. Nothing more.

In other words, she needed my help, but she'd tell me when, where, and what. She should have realized when she'd confided in me that I struggled with boundaries. I got that from my mother.

But I didn't want to risk losing the tentative partnership that the sheriff and I had, so back to the rec room I went. Except, the room was empty when I arrived.

I pulled my phone from my purse and glanced at the screen. Dinnertime.

Navigation of the spaceport was still a struggle. Even after several days there, I hadn't yet figured out how to get to the staff dorms from this side of the building. But the cafeteria was one location I'd mastered the path to, no matter where I was starting from.

Sure enough, when I arrived, the astronauts were there, piling up their food and settling in at one of the long school-cafeteria-style tables.

A quick scan showed that Ace was missing. Probably being questioned by the sheriff. Whitney was heading over from the Thai section. Emma sat at the end of the table with a salad, while Noah slid in across from her with a plate stacked high with pizza. Eating seemed to be his activity of choice for the week, considering he hadn't participated in much of anything else.

"Where's Rachel?" I asked, suddenly realizing she wasn't there either. The sheriff had said she'd finished questioning her, and she should have made it here before me.

As soon as I asked, and every gaze in the room landed on me, I realized I had once again made the mistake of acting as if I were a part of their group. Even so, Noah answered.

"She and Emma had a fight, so she went back to the dorms."

Emma shot him a glare, apparently not liking that he

was sharing insider information with me, but he ignored her.

"I'm sure emotions are running high, considering the circumstances," I said, setting my purse and the camera down at the opposite end of the table. I wanted to be close enough to have a conversation but far enough away that I wouldn't be considered presumptuous. "Anyone know how soon we get to leave tomorrow? The earlier, the better."

I asked as if I didn't work there—as if I didn't have a personal relationship with the sheriff. Well, as personal as she'd allow it to be.

The others didn't buy it. Whitney snorted as he plopped down onto the bench. "Sorry, Doc, but we're not going to be spilling our guts to you in an impromptu group therapy session. Last thing we need is to be splashed across the gossip columns."

Emma shook her head. "Please. You spread rumors about yourself to end up in those columns, Whitney."

The comment didn't faze the actor. He raised his shoulder. "I got to do something to stay relevant, don't I? But being connected to your mother's murder wouldn't exactly help my career." His gaze found its way back to me. "Even so, if we did know who took out the fashion queen, it wouldn't be you that we'd confess it to."

I leaned forward and rested my elbows on the table. "Who would you confess it to? A priest? We could arrange for one to drive out." I gave him a smile that I hoped conveyed I was kidding. Mostly.

Whitney snorted and shoved a forkful of curry into his mouth. "Look, Doc, these have been a trying few days," he said around the mouthful of food. "We didn't choose our traveling companions, but from the looks of things, someone else did. Charlotte's murder proves it. So maybe stop accusing us and take a closer look at who orchestrated everything."

If Whitney had wanted to shock me, he'd succeeded. I didn't know what to say to that.

He was saying there was a reason that the seven of them had been put on the same flight. I hadn't ever considered that and assumed that everyone was placed on the flight in the order they'd purchased their seats. Galactic Enterprises had been pre-selling tickets for years as they worked to make space tourism a reality.

My surprise must have been obvious because he smirked and went back to eating. I was being played. That was what actors did, right? I would have left it at that if it weren't for Emma. I glanced her way to see what she thought of Whitney's insinuation. She shrugged and then avoided my gaze, but it was her eyes that troubled me. Before she had looked away, I'd sworn I'd seen panic in them. Fear.

And guilt.

It was easier to assume that Whitney was messing with me.

But what if I was wrong?

Rushing from the cafeteria at that moment to pay the

sheriff a visit would have been a bit obvious, so I wandered over to the Mexican side of the cafeteria. I tried to look like I was having a difficult time making up my mind about which dish to choose, when really I was lost in my own thoughts.

Ace arrived in the cafeteria not long after Whitney had made his declaration, and it was only another ten minutes before the sheriff called Whitney out for questioning. He seemed nervous as he was led out, but I had been in his shoes before, and the anxiety of being questioned by law enforcement never diminished. It was always terrifying, even if you were innocent.

I'd finally decided on enchiladas when I heard a shout from the hallway.

Julie stuck her head into the cafeteria, her brow creased in worry, though her voice was firm and commanding. "Dr. Swallows. I need you out here. Now."

"If you'd return my phone, then you'd be able to get ahold of me easier," I said for the benefit of the group. They didn't know mine had been returned.

The look Julie gave me, though, like if I said one more word she would lose it, silenced me. I hurried out after her, ignoring the curious glances of the others. Emma and Ace followed us out at a distance, likely wondering what the commotion was.

"Maddie Swallows," someone was calling from around the corner of the hallway. Sounded like it was in the direction of the entryway, but it was difficult to tell. "Maddie, this is your mother speaking. Tell them I'm allowed to be here."

I looked to Julie, not bothering to mask my horror. "You said she wouldn't make it this far."

Julie raised her hands in a defensive gesture as she speed-walked down the hallway, and I quickened my steps to keep up with her. "She shouldn't have been able to. It seems I underestimated your mother's elderly charm and overestimated my security guards' ability to properly do their job."

"I'm not elderly," a voice yelled. "Sixty-five isn't old."

Heat rushed into my cheeks, and it felt like when I was a teenager all over again. I'd been mortified at my mother's behavior on a daily basis—she'd never had the ability to do anything quietly.

We rounded the corner into the hallway where the administration offices were and stopped outside Julie's office. My mother was standing at Julie's desk, but I had no idea where Flash and Lilly were.

"Mom, I told you you're not allowed here," I said, entering. "They could have you arrested, you know."

My mom waved a hand through the air and scoffed. "Danielle Potts already tried."

I threw Julie a bewildered look, and her gaze rose to the ceiling, as if she were praying.

"That's when I came and got you, Maddie," Julie said, her gaze returning to me. "The sheriff received an urgent phone call and left me to deal with it."

This was ridiculous. I turned on my mom. "Where are the kids?"

My mom nodded toward the security doors that led from the hallway to the lobby. "Can you believe they refused to leave the security desk? Since when did they become rule-followers? If anyone were to break into this place, I'd think it would be them."

"You are not helping your case," I yelped, fighting the urge to bury my head in my hands and call it quits. "Mom, not only are you not allowed to be here, but we are in the middle of a murder investigation. You have to go home."

My mom narrowed her eyes. "Or what?"

"Or I will arrest you myself." I knew it was a dumb thing to say. I had no authority to arrest anyone, let alone my own mother. Before anyone could tell me as much, I added, "A citizen's arrest."

Was that how that worked? I had no idea.

But it had the desired effect.

My mom immediately backed down. Except, I hadn't anticipated the moisture in her eyes. The sudden defeat that seemed to wash over her. The hurt.

I released a long sigh. "Mom, I'm sorry. I didn't mean that. But I'm concerned about your recklessness, especially when you drag my kids into it with you." The fact that they had refused to come any further gave me hope that, despite their sometimes questionable activities, they knew which lines not to cross.

She gave a small nod. "I just wanted to help—to protect

my only daughter. A mother's love is something you can't understand until you experience it for yourself."

I was unsure if she was directing that comment toward me or Julie, but when my mom's gaze landed on me, it left me spluttering. "Mom, if you hadn't noticed, I have two children whom I love very much. But that doesn't mean I have carte blanche to do whatever I want."

My mom stood and patted my shoulder, as if she felt sorry for me. I stared, aghast, as she said, "I suppose that's where I went wrong with you. Didn't teach you properly." She gave a defeated sigh. "Fine. We'll leave. If that is what you want."

"Actually, you won't," Sheriff Potts said, appearing in the doorway. "Consider the spaceport sealed until tomorrow at the astronauts' scheduled departure time."

"What?" Julie and I said simultaneously as my mother beamed at the two of us.

"Well, would you look at that. Looks like they do need our help, after all." My mom's voice dropped to an offended mumble. "Even if my own daughter doesn't."

Sheriff Potts gave me a look that told me she didn't like this any more than I did, and then turned her gaze to Julie. "Your employees come in from all over the country for these flights, not to mention your astronauts. We have new information that leads us to believe that if the killer leaves the spaceport, we'll never see them again."

"What information?" Julie asked, her tone rising as she took a step forward.

The sheriff looked like she was about to answer, but then she stopped short. "I'm sorry, I'm not able to share that at this time."

Julie's furrowed brow popped up in surprise. "I thought you found the murder weapon under one of the astronauts' seats. That they are being detained. Are you telling me you think you have the wrong person?"

"I don't know," Sheriff Potts said, her words slow. "But I don't believe that astronaut could have been working alone. And these seven astronauts were not chosen at random." She paused. "They had an inside man. Or woman."

12

I hadn't shared with the sheriff what Whitney had told me—about the astronauts not being chosen at random. So how had the sheriff come to the same conclusion? Unless Whitney had shared his theory with the sheriff when she'd called him out, but I had a difficult time believing he'd be so forthcoming. He didn't seem the type.

"I need to go let the kids know what's going on," I said, reaching for my purse. Except, it wasn't there. I must have left it, along with Jeffrey's camera, in the cafeteria when Julie had pulled me out. I turned to my mom. "I forgot my stuff, but you need to stay put until I get back. You can't go wandering around without a security badge."

Her lips pulled down into a frown. "You don't have to treat me like a child, you know. It's insulting."

"Then maybe you shouldn't go breaking into places, expecting me to bail you out."

My mom's frown deepened. I had hurt her feelings. Again.

"I'm sorry, Mom. I am. But this job is important to me, and you've put me in a very awkward position."

She sighed and her forehead smoothed. "You're right," she conceded. "But I'm only here because I wanted to help."

I kissed her on top of her head. "I know. Be back in a minute, and then we'll see if we can convince the sheriff to let you guys sneak out so you can go back home." I threw a glance at Sheriff Potts, but she didn't give any indication of whether that would be possible. Instead, she followed me out of Julie's office and shut the door.

"Is everything okay?" I asked. Other than her sealing off the entire spaceport and trapping my family here until further notice.

The sheriff stayed quiet for a moment, pursing her lips, as if trying to decide how much to tell me. "I need you to leave your purse where it is for now."

I cocked one eyebrow. "You do know it has my phone in it, right?"

"I didn't. But it's a risk I'm willing to take."

Sheriff Potts wasn't always forthright with me about her investigations, but she was never sneaky. If she didn't want me nosing around—which had been one hundred percent of the time before today—she'd tell me. She didn't play games, and I'd always appreciated that about her.

Until now.

She was being secretive, and it left me with the distinct feeling that I was being used as a pawn in a game that I didn't understand.

"How did you come to the conclusion that this whole trip was orchestrated?" I asked. "You think these seven astronauts were chosen for a purpose and that one of them is working with an inside person. Why?"

Guilt flashed across the sheriff's face. It was gone just as quickly as it had arrived, but it had been enough.

My purse.

"You've been spying," I whispered, walking quickly past the sheriff. When she'd said she wanted me to be her eyes and ears, I'd thought she needed the skills I'd honed over many years of being a licensed therapist. I'd felt needed. Turned out I'd been used. Betrayed. There was a reason she didn't want me to retrieve my purse, and I was fairly certain I knew what it was.

Sheriff Potts waited a beat before hurrying after me, cutting me off just before I reached the security doors that would lead into the heart of the spaceport. "Fine. Yes. I planted a listening device in your purse."

"That's how you got to the rec room so quickly when the others discovered I still had my phone." It was all coming together. And I didn't like it. My eyebrows furrowed. "But it's not just their conversations you've been listening to. You've been listening to mine as well. How long has it been there?"

I scanned my memory, trying to remember everything

that had gone on since the sheriff had arrived. She must have known my mom was coming because I'd had that conversation in the cafeteria. And she hadn't said anything. Hadn't sealed the spaceport before they arrived.

"I placed it when I pulled you out to interrogate you, right after I arrived," she admitted. "And you forgetting your purse in the cafeteria is the best thing that's happened for my investigation. As soon as you left, the floodgates opened. The celebrities all have theories on who the killer was, what happened, and I have to say, the theories are all viable. Once my deputy gives me a call telling me they've finished, you can retrieve your purse."

Questions. So many questions. But I couldn't single any one of them out. Because the only thing I felt in that moment was anger.

"Why didn't you stop my family from coming when you knew they were on their way?" I asked. "You could have sealed off the spaceport ten minutes earlier, rather than trapping them here."

A brief flicker of doubt. "Honestly, I didn't think they'd be able to get past security. This is an active murder investigation, after all. And you'd already warned Julie. What could I have done that was any different?"

"You mean you didn't want to reveal that you'd been spying."

She raised a shoulder. "That too."

"Gah." I threw my arms in the air. "I can't believe you'd do this to me. I don't care if the celebrities are still in the cafeteria. I don't even care if one of them is in the middle of a confession. I'm getting my purse, and you can say goodbye to your bug."

I turned on my heel and scanned my security badge at the door that would allow me to retrieve my belongings, and then I would be escorting my family off the premises.

The light blinked red, indicating that I didn't have access.

I tried again. More red.

"What did you do?" I demanded, spinning back toward Sheriff Potts.

She held out her hands in a defensive gesture. "I disabled everyone's security access for the entrances and exits in this section of the building."

"But—"

Sheriff Potts spoke over me. "For the next twenty-four hours, if you want to go somewhere that requires additional clearance, you need to be escorted there by Julie, Dr. Randall, Officer Bridge, or myself."

"You don't have a right to do that. You either need to charge me with murder or allow me and my family to leave the spaceport—I'm done here." At least, that was how it always worked in those TV shows. I assumed those writers had done their research.

"I'm not holding you hostage. Tomorrow you will return home as planned, per your contract with the spaceport."

Stupid contract.

"Then let my family go."

Sheriff Potts gave a single nod. "Fine. They are free to go, and I will personally escort them out to ensure their safety." She held up one finger. "*If* they want to, that is."

"If they—" Realization washed over me. Oh, she was good. "I can't believe this," I said with a laugh of disbelief. "You want them here. That's the real reason you didn't seal off the spaceport earlier. You know my family puts themselves neck deep where they shouldn't be, and they have no qualms getting involved in things that you have to stay out of. You want to use them, and you can't come right out and ask." I shook my head. "What happened to the rule-following sheriff I met when we first moved to Amor? The one who wouldn't ever consider planting bugs on the local psychologist or using teenagers as part of her murder investigation?"

The sheriff released a long sigh and leaned against the wall. "She realized that she's stuck in the small town of Amor forever, that she's never getting out, and that no one wants her job, so she's never getting fired." When she saw my shocked expression, she hurriedly added, "I haven't given up on myself completely. But sometimes things need to be done to bring people to justice that I don't have access to. Or don't have time to wait for."

I pointed a finger at Sheriff Potts. "I won't let you use them to do your dirty work."

She gave a vigorous nod. "And I don't want them to. Honest."

"That being said," I said, my words slow, "when Flash called to warn me that they were on their way, he did mention that he has some information on the murder victim that we might be interested in."

Sheriff Potts straightened. "Really."

"And if someone, perhaps local law enforcement, happened to overhear as Flash told me about it...well, I have no control over that."

"I suppose not." The sheriff hesitated. "Look, Maddie. I would never be able to use any of the information I obtained from the listening device in court. It was just to help me figure out where to start looking. I have less than twenty-four hours before most of the spaceport empties out and the astronauts board a plane for home. I can't risk losing the murderer. Not when so much is on the line for everyone involved."

Looking at Sheriff Potts, for a brief moment I could see the woman behind the badge. The one who had come to Amor with no family and no friends. The woman who had been forced to come to our small town because she had been wrongly accused of a crime she hadn't committed. Though no one could prove she'd done it, she was being punished all the same.

And now, after three years in Amor, she still had no friends in our closed-minded town. Everyone saw her as an outsider. An enforcer. Not someone you wanted to get close to.

It had to be so lonely.

"Danielle," I started. I'd never called the sheriff by her first name before, and it felt strange on my tongue. The sheriff's eyes narrowed briefly, and I paused, immediately regretting my choice. But then her expression relaxed and one corner of her lips pulled up.

"Yes?"

Hmm. Maybe now that we were more like partners in this investigation, and she'd dragged my entire family into it, it was okay.

Maybe we were even becoming...dare I say it...friends.

"We will help you in any way we can," I said. "And you know my mom and the kids will be on board. But you have to be honest with us. No more sneaking around."

Danielle was already nodding before I'd finished speaking. "You have my word."

Great. Now that that was out of the way. "About my security badge..."

"Nope. It will be too suspicious if yours is the only one that works."

I gave her what I hoped was an innocent smile. "I had to try, didn't I?"

She laughed. "You wouldn't be Maddie Swallows if you didn't."

Julie's office door opened, and my mom stuck her head out. She frowned when she saw the sheriff and me at the end of the hallway. "You're still here? You were supposed to get your purse and come back for me."

"My badge doesn't work anymore," I said with a help-less shrug. I passed it over the scanner to prove it.

My mom was too smart for that. "Whatever plan you two are hatching, you better share it. You're useless without me and the kids."

She'd always been convinced that my degrees in psychology had been a waste of time—that I'd gained nothing from all those years slaving away at the university.

"You can't keep a secret," I said. "You'll give everything away."

"I will not," she huffed. "And to prove that I can be helpful, I'm going to figure out why Charlotte didn't leave any of her inheritance to her daughter, Emma."

I did not know that little piece of information. One glance at Danielle told me she didn't either.

"Where did you hear that from?" I asked. "You just got here."

My mom smiled wickedly. "I can keep a secret when I want to. Guess you gotta keep me around now." She called to Julie over her shoulder. "Looks like I'm staying."

And then she sauntered out in front of us, glancing back impatiently as she waited for someone to open the security door.

This investigation had just gotten a lot more interesting.

13

"And this is where you'll be staying tonight," I said as I swung open the door to our room. Even though it housed three bunk beds, I'd been by myself. Originally Lilly was going to be staying with me, but when she had been replaced with Jeffrey, they had moved him in with Dr. Randall so I would have privacy.

I was infinitely grateful for the kind gesture.

"This is so cool," Flash said, throwing his backpack on the top bunk closest to the window. "I can't believe they're letting us stay."

Neither could I. But here we were.

"I think your grandma just wore them down until they were tired of saying no," I said, throwing my mom an amused yet slightly annoyed look. I hoped she interpreted it as such.

Lilly tossed her bag under her brother's bed. "That,

and I heard the sheriff managed to convince that Julie lady that we would be less trouble if she agreed to let us stay."

Flash grinned and released a dramatic sigh. "The sheriff knows us so well."

"She knows you better than she should," I said, placing my purse on the built-in desk next to my bed. When I'd returned to the cafeteria to retrieve it, the tables had been full and my purse shoved unceremoniously under one of them. And there had been no camera. I hoped I could find it before the sheriff realized I'd lost it. Jeffrey had taken so many pictures, I'd only made it through half of them.

My gaze lingered on the small electronic device fastened to the inside lining of my purse. "So, before we head to bed, I need to know what you three know that I don't."

The kids and my mom all shared glances, conveying messages that I couldn't understand. Like they'd formed a secret spy club while I'd been away.

My mom was the first to speak. "We have no way of knowing what you don't know, dear. You'll have to be more specific."

After all that drama, they had the audacity to be cagey with me. "Nope. That's not how this is going to go. You don't get to pretend that you don't know what I'm talking about. Not when you threw yourselves smack dab in the middle of a murder investigation, or put another way, you decided you wanted to spend the evening in the same building as a killer." I threw a glance at my mom. "Thanks for that, by the way. As if I don't worry about my kids enough."

She gave me the innocent grandmotherly expression that had probably gotten her past the security guards. "I missed you."

I snorted. "Uh huh. Right. So, you just happened to already know all about the fashion icon Charlotte Fischer's inheritance plans before embarking on a road trip to see your daughter, who you missed so much."

"Might as well come clean," Flash said. "She already knows I have some information."

"Me too," my mom conceded.

Lilly released an exasperated sigh. "Am I the only one who stuck to the plan? She can't send us home if we have information she needs."

"Don't worry, you'll get your autograph," Flash said, rolling his eyes. "Grandma promised."

I turned on my mom. "You promised her an autograph by Ace Hutchins? We all signed a ton of forms that specifically said we wouldn't ask for that kind of thing. This is his vacation, and he doesn't deserve to be swarmed by fans."

"Fan. Singular," Flash said. "I don't want one. And Grandma also promised her one by Rachel what's-her-name."

Lilly turned an annoyed look on her brother. "How many times do I have to tell you that it's Rachel Sinclair?"

I massaged my brow. "For right now, can we focus on whatever information you three are withholding from me?

The sooner you do, the quicker we can get you guys some dinner. The cafeteria closes at seven."

That caught Flash's attention, as I'd known it would. "You mean...we get to eat at the cafeteria you told me about? Where you can eat as much as you want, and you don't have to pay?"

"I don't have to pay," I corrected him. "Because I actually work here. For you, on the other hand, they'll probably charge by the ounce."

I knew they wouldn't, because they had no way of accepting payment, but Flash didn't know that.

It turned out that he didn't care whether he'd have to pay. "I have plenty of money."

That he did. I'd never known how lucrative computer hacking could be until my teenage son started winning competitions. It worried me how good he was at it.

Flash glanced at his phone, probably checking how long he had until closing time, then slipped it back into his pocket. "Okay," he said, his words quick. Must have been getting close to seven. "Charlotte has changed her will three times in the past year. The most recent time was two weeks ago."

That wasn't long at all. I wondered what had prompted the change. "I'm assuming Emma gets everything?"

Flash shook his head. "The opposite. Emma gets nothing. Charlotte left all her money to some charitable organization that rescues beagles from animal testing sites."

Oh, that was cute. Weird that someone would leave

their fortune to it and cut their own daughter out of the will. How many beagles were being subjected to testing at any single moment?

"So, two weeks ago something happens that makes Charlotte so furious that she cuts her daughter out of the will."

"Wrong again," he said. "Emma was never inheriting her mom's fortune. Before the change, some psychic was getting it all. Can't remember her name." He looked at me eagerly, as if he were wondering if he'd done well enough to deserve to go to dinner.

Despite my insides churning, I smiled and nodded. "Let's get you three something to eat."

Hopefully Sheriff Danielle Potts had gotten all that. And if she had any further questions, she'd know where to find us.

THANKFULLY, the cafeteria was nearly empty when we arrived. A couple of stray employees were just finishing up, but by the time we'd loaded up our trays, they'd left.

And when I said my family loaded up their trays, that was not an exaggeration. Flash had three plates on his tray, and he ate like he'd never seen food before.

"You're disgusting," Lilly said, shooting him a look of repulsion. Of course, she had one plate that held four slices of pizza, one bowl filled with curry, and then another plate for enchiladas. At least she was somewhat civilized as she ate, and even managed to use a napkin.

The same couldn't be said of her brother.

"So, who are your primary suspects?" Flash asked around a mouthful of food. I tried to not look as a piece of chicken fell out and onto the plate.

I took a bite of my spaghetti and chewed thoughtfully. "I don't know. Everything points to Serena. Sheriff Potts has her confined to a small library near my office. Has Officer Bridge standing guard and everything."

"Who's Serena again?" my mom asked.

"The psychic." I pushed away my spaghetti, leaving it only half-eaten. I'd never have thought it possible, but I wasn't hungry. "The murder had to be premeditated. Serena didn't just find the knife on board and think, *What should I do with this? Oh, I know, I'll kill the woman who recently cut me out of her will.*" I paused. "I know it makes sense that she did it, but I don't believe Serena is a murderer."

"Besides, it's too obvious," Lilly said, pointing her fork at me. "I mean, Serena predicts Charlotte's death before she actually does it, and then hides the murder weapon under her own seat? If you had planned the whole thing out, why would you do that?"

Flash took a swig of his soda. "Maybe something went wrong and she had to hide the knife quicker than she'd expected."

"Except, you said all of these people might have been

brought together for a purpose," Lilly said. "Who has the power to do that? Certainly not a celebrity psychic."

I had no idea. And what would bringing all of them together accomplish? As soon as I asked myself, I knew.

Six people with motive. Figuring out which one had done it would be next to impossible. And if you knew that one person stood to gain more than the others, that was your fall guy. The killer didn't know Serena had been cut out of the will. This flight had been planned for months.

"What about Ace?" I mused.

Lilly's eyes widened a fraction, and she gave her head a vigorous shake. "No. Don't you dare. Ace Hutchins is a beautiful human being and he's off limits."

I gave her an apologetic smile. "All seven of these astronauts were brought together to create high emotions. Confusion. Make things messy. Emma must have been angry with her mother, being treated the way she was, especially if she knew she wasn't receiving any of the inheritance. Maybe she was even angrier with Serena and wanted to see the blame fall on her. Rachel was upset with Charlotte for never giving her a chance. Whitney blames both Serena and Ace for his lackluster career, and there may be a connection we don't know about between him and Charlotte."

"What about the quiet nerd you were telling us about? There has to be a boatload of suppressed rage just begging to come out. Maybe it finally did," Lilly said, seeming desperate to pin it on anyone other than her beloved Ace Hutchins.

Charlotte did seem to have that effect on people, but Noah didn't interact with anyone. Didn't participate. Just quietly did his thing, like he was biding his time until he could go home. Didn't even seem like he wanted to be at the spaceport.

So, why was he?

"No one is above suspicion," I conceded.

I was unsure if Sheriff Potts had been listening in on our lunchtime conversation. She had to have better things to do with her time, and I'd nearly convinced myself of it before my conversation with the kids was interrupted by Officer Bridge entering the cafeteria, his gaze zeroing in on me. It turned out, however, that he wasn't there on the sheriff's behalf.

"Have you seen Danielle?" he asked.

My eyebrows popped up in surprise, and I shared an amused look with my mom. Either the sheriff and Officer Bridge had known each other previously or they'd arrived at first-name status rather quickly. I was barely moving into that territory and had known the sheriff for a couple of years now.

My gaze returned to Officer Bridge. "I have not. Have you tried my office?"

He gave a slow nod. "Yes, that was the first place I looked. Maybe she's in the secure wing interviewing the engineers."

"Is there something we can help you with?" my mom asked with a slight smile.

A blush crept up the officer's neck, and he took a step back. "Just needed to...ask her something." He turned his gaze to me. "It's about you, actually. Serena is requesting a therapy session. Thought I should get Danielle's permission first."

"I can give you the sheriff's phone number, if that would be easier. In all honesty, though, I'm going to head over to the library and speak with Serena, with or without *Danielle's* permission."

Officer Bridge gave his head a vigorous shake. "I already have her number, and you really should wait until I get ahold of her." He paused, the pink of his neck darkening to crimson. "I'll let you know when I have the go-ahead." And then he hurried out.

My mom and the kids exchanged curious glances, and a snicker escaped Lilly. "Does Officer Bridge have a thing for the sheriff?"

"Looked like it to me," my mom said. "Bet he was just looking for an excuse to go see her."

Flash scrunched up his nose. "Gross."

I laughed, but I could see where Officer Bridge was coming from. I'd always known Sheriff Potts in an official capacity, but without the uniform and constant stress that came with the job, they might make a cute couple.

"Even if it was just an excuse, I better check on Serena and make sure everything is okay. This is my job—what

I'm paid to do. And Sheriff Potts doesn't have the right to stop me from doing it." I paused. "You three going to be okay for an hour?" I was more concerned what they would do without my supervision.

Flash shoved in three more bites of food and stood with his now-empty plates. "That depends," he said, mouth still full. "Can we play the arcades?"

I hesitated. The rec room was likely where the astronauts were. Ever since the disastrous flight, they'd basically claimed it as theirs. I didn't think they'd be rude to my mom and the kids, but chances were that a murderer hid among them. Not exactly a scenario I was thrilled with.

My mom answered before I had the chance. "Of course you can. I heard they have a pool table, and if you get hungry again, they have snacks."

She knew just what buttons to push.

"I'll walk you there. It can be easy to get lost in this place," I said, wanting to check out the room first. Make sure they'd be okay. That they wouldn't be murdered.

My mom gave me an exasperated look. "Serena needs you, and you don't need to be wasting your time on us. We'll find it with no problem, and you can meet us there when you're finished."

I hesitated. "Okay. If you're sure."

"It's like she doesn't trust us," she said to the kids, escorting them out.

Yeah, it was like that.

I was the last to leave the cafeteria, and I made my way

to the library. Because of its proximity to my office, it made it easy for the sheriff to keep an eye on her prime suspect.

I approached the door but then hesitated. Officer Bridge wasn't back yet, and the door was slightly ajar.

My pulse quickened when I drew closer and heard two distinct voices inside. I paused, leaning in to try to hear better.

"Do you think they suspect?" Serena said.

A laugh. "No, and they're too worried about themselves to care. Wouldn't change anything, anyway."

Most people at the spaceport wouldn't recognize the man's voice because they hadn't been given the opportunity to hear it.

But I knew exactly who I'd discover when I opened the door.

"Well, doesn't this look cozy," I said, walking into the room.

14

S erena glanced up from the overstuffed chair she sat in, her legs dangling over the armrest. "Oh, good. Sheriff Potts allowed you to come."

I looked to Noah, who stood by a large bookcase. He wasn't startled by my presence, and in fact seemed like he'd been expecting me.

"Are we doing a couples session?" I asked, pointing to Noah.

"Something like that." Serena smiled, not at all looking like the prime suspect in a murder case.

I bounced my gaze between Serena and Noah, attempting to make sense of the current situation.

Serena nodded to the chair across from her. "Please, sit."

"O-kay." I dutifully crossed the room and took my place, though unsure why.

"Dr. Swallows, I didn't murder Charlotte."

Noah nodded in agreement.

"You would make a terrible murderer if you had," I said.

Serena grinned and looked to Noah. "See, I told you she could help us."

I hesitated, feeling like I'd once again entered a game that I hadn't agreed to play. "I'm not here to determine guilt or innocence, Serena. I'm here to help you process any difficult feelings you might be having. Beyond that, it's the sheriff you need to be talking to."

Though I had to admit to being curious about what part Noah played in all of this.

"The thing is," Noah said, "from Sheriff Potts' point of view, Serena is guilty. She's thought it from the beginning. But it's simply not true."

"That prediction I made," Serena said. "It wasn't about Charlotte's death. It was referring to the death of her company. She was one week away from losing her business, and then she would have been obsolete. No one would be talking about her or her dresses anymore. Not without a miracle." She paused. "Sheriff Potts told me about the inheritance. I swear, I had no idea. Charlotte never told me. Even if she had, it wouldn't be something to kill her over. There was nothing left to inherit."

I studied the duo in front of me, still unsure what Noah had to do with anything and wondering if Serena could be trusted.

My gut said no.

"I suppose you gleaned this information from one of your visions?" I said, leaning back in the chair.

Serena shook her head. "No. I went to Charlotte's for a reading a couple of months ago, but the energy in the room was chaotic and I couldn't connect with her the way I had been able to in the past. That was when she told me about her financial troubles and how she couldn't confide in anyone, least of all Emma. The girl was bleeding Charlotte dry, living off her the way she was."

"Why didn't she just cut Emma off?"

Noah answered for Serena. "Because, whatever your impressions of the girl, Emma isn't the type to go quietly. You can ask Whitney; he knows a thing or two about that. And then the world would suspect what was really going on behind Charlotte's closed doors. She hoped her next fashion show that was scheduled for next month would help put an end to her troubles and no one would be the wiser."

I shot him a skeptical glance. "And you know this how? Just from first impressions, you don't seem the type who has need of a celebrity psychic."

Serena and Noah shared a look where an entire unspoken conversation happened in a matter of seconds. They didn't have to tell me what this meant.

"You're romantically involved," I said, unable to hide my shock. They'd gone to great lengths to hide their connection.

"No," Serena said, quickly denying the obvious conclusion. "He's my brother." She paused. "And our father owns Galactic Enterprises. Our dad is Ted Carson."

Whatever my shock had been before, it had just multiplied. Noah's missing last name in his file made sense now. Julie had to have known and been under direct instructions that no one else find out. Serena was using her psychic name, so she wasn't at risk of being found out.

And now I understood why Ted Carson was calling Sheriff Potts every five minutes, demanding updates.

"It's all very complicated," Noah said when I remained silent, attempting to wrap my head around everything that was happening. "But suffice to say, my sister and I live very different lives. The one thing we have in common is that we want nothing to do with the family business. My sister is successful in ways that our father disapproves of, and I'm unsuccessful in every way, unless you're measuring happiness, which our father does not."

I held out my hands, gesturing around me. "So...what are you doing here? At the spaceport."

Serena and Noah shared the look again—the one that was so familiar I'd mistaken it for romance.

"We don't know," Serena finally answered. "We didn't sign on for the flight. When we confronted our father, he swore he had nothing to do with us being here. It would be the type of thing he'd do—try and convince us to forsake our current paths and join the family business by sending us to space. He did admit to placing our names on the waiting list so that if we ever changed our minds, he could put us on the next flight."

I crossed my legs to keep them from bouncing. They did that when I was anxious. "You didn't have to show up."

"We were...curious," Noah said, his words slow. "Cautious, but curious. A car showed up at each of our homes the day we were meant to leave. A car that we didn't request. Even though we knew we were likely playing into our father's manipulative hands, we thought it might get him off our backs if we said we'd given it a fair shot."

Serena snorted. "We were playing into someone's hands all right."

As a psychic, Serena had been surprised by a lot of unexpected events these past few days. I felt like she should have seen them coming.

"I can't see the future," she said, as if reading my mind. It sent chills through me, and I reminded myself that I didn't believe in psychics. "I do own a crystal ball, but that is what people expect. What I *can* do is tap into the energy of a room or the energy of a specific person. This helps me to access their subconscious and then guide them onto the best path forward. And yes, I can sometimes tap into the future of that person. But it's not like a movie projector. So you can imagine my shock to see Charlotte, Emma, and the rest of the gang at that little hotel in Amor where we were meant to catch the shuttle out here."

"The rest of the gang?" I asked, leaning forward. Psychic or not, this had been the most valuable therapy session I'd had yet. I glanced at the floor, expecting to see my purse and the listening device.

It wasn't there. Danielle wasn't hearing a word of this.

"Your purse is with your mother in the recreation room," Serena said, her lips pulling into a smile.

How did that happen? I'd consciously kept it with me since forgetting it in the cafeteria.

Serena leaned forward, matching my stance. "I know about the device—it interferes with the energy of a room. I've known the entire time, and I needed to be able to speak freely. Without listening ears."

My blood chilled. Why couldn't I remember where I'd last seen my purse? Had Noah snatched it and placed it elsewhere?

"We don't mean you any harm," Noah said, reading my discomfort. "But we don't know who we can trust. We can't trust even the sheriff. That entire group of astronauts out there is the underbelly of the celebrity world. Serena would know because she's worked with all of them."

I pulled in a long breath. Everything was fine. I glanced toward the door, but it didn't appear that Officer Bridge had returned. Either that or he wasn't concerned about what we were doing.

"He knows who our dad is," Serena said, her gaze following mine. "Officer Bridge. And yet he still felt the need to get the sheriff's permission for this little chat. Worked to our advantage, didn't it."

Serena and Noah seemed like the type of people who knew how to make someone disappear. How long would it be until my family thought to come looking for me? An hour at least.

Noah released a long breath. "Seriously, we're the good guys. We're the only ones who chose to visit with you in your office, right?"

I nodded. "You were scoping things out. Trying to get a read on me."

"As soon as we saw who was gathered here for our flight, we knew something was up," Serena said. "And we needed to know who we could confide in." She paused. "You're it. The only one."

Flattery wasn't going to get them very far. I stood. "You are working hard to make me feel important. But you haven't told me a thing. Whatever conspiracy you think is happening, tell it to the sheriff. Because I'm tired of being used and lied to. My family is here now—my kids and my mom. That is where my focus will be until we're able to leave tomorrow."

I hadn't thought Serena capable of murder. I still wasn't convinced. But my drive to find who had really killed Charlotte was disappearing fast. I just wanted to get out of there.

"Dr. Swallows is right," Noah said to his sister. "She has

no reason to trust us. Not when we're throwing all this stuff at her." He then turned to me. "We appreciate you coming by and listening as long as you did. When you leave, for the sake of your family, please remember one thing. Everyone on that flight—they are professional liars. And they've all done terrible things to achieve success. Everything from bribes and blackmail to sleeping with the right people. You don't want your family mixed up with them."

"Even Ace?" I asked, remembering how smitten Lilly was with the actor.

Serena grimaced. "Especially Ace. These celebrities say they rely on my psychic abilities for their success, but they twist my predictions and apply them in ways they weren't meant to be." She looked at the floor, her curly hair obscuring her face. "They take things too far. I advised Whitney not to accept the part that launched Ace's career because I was afraid for Whitney."

My breath caught in my chest, and I had to force myself to breathe again.

"I'll keep that in mind," I said, taking a step toward the door. "Thank you."

Serena stood. "Please don't judge me too harshly. Two months ago, I told each of the people who are sitting in the rec room that I was no longer going to be working with them. Everyone except Charlotte. And staying with her as long as I did was a mistake."

"So, why weren't you the one with the knife in your side?" I asked, still skeptical about everything I was being told. Like her brother had said, they were all professional liars. "You know everything about all of them and were about to walk away."

"I don't know, but I hope you figure it out before I end up like Charlotte."

15

My head swam as I attempted to make sense of everything. No one was what they appeared to be in this place. And if Serena's intuition was anything to go by, it wasn't just the astronauts we needed to be worried about. Yes, one of them had killed Charlotte, but how had they gotten the knife in the first place?

And why?

Charlotte had been close to bankruptcy. Which meant she had needed money. Maybe she had been blackmailing the others. That might warrant a knife in the side.

I leaned against the wall in the hallway and squeezed my eyes shut. My family shouldn't be here. *I* shouldn't be here.

After checking in with my family, I needed to relay what I had learned to Danielle. Once I did, it would no longer be my burden to carry.

When I arrived at the rec room, however, only one person was there.

Emma.

She was sitting by herself at the snack bar, but she wasn't eating anything. Just sitting. Staring. Emma turned when the door closed with a loud thud.

"I'm sorry," I said, not moving further into the room. "I was just looking for my kids."

It took a long moment for my words to register. When they finally seemed to click, she said, "Everyone went back to the dorms. Even Whitney, who never goes to bed before three in the morning. Guess there's something about murder that makes everyone tired and want to tuck in early."

I took a hesitant step toward the artist. No matter what she'd done in the past to get where she was now, she needed a listening ear. Someone who wouldn't tell her that everything would be all right or that her mother was in a better place. She needed someone who would just allow her to be sad.

"Emma—" I started.

She held up a hand. "I'm not in the mood right now, Doc. I don't want to talk about my complicated relationship with my mom, and I certainly don't want to speculate about who I think might have murdered her."

I gave a little nod and turned back toward the door. "Just for the record," I said over my shoulder, "when I say I'm sorry, I mean it. And when I say you are welcome to talk to me anytime between now and when we leave tomorrow, it means I hope you take me up on it."

And then I left Emma to think on it.

I sure hoped she wasn't the one who had murdered her mom.

I APPROACHED THE STAFF DORMS, exhausted and wishing I could go to bed, regardless of how early it was. Just outside the door, I paused. Something didn't feel right.

"Let go," Lilly screeched from inside our room.

The killer. They were here.

I burst through the door, armed with...nothing. I didn't have my purse, or my dog repellent, or anything remotely heavy. I wasn't even armed with muscles. As often as I'd become involved in murder investigations, weightlifting really should have become a priority by now.

But there was no murderer in the room. Only a teenage boy huddled in the corner of the top bunk, holding a large photograph just out of Lilly's reach. My mom sat in a chair on the opposite end of the room, reading while wearing headphones.

"Flash, give whatever that is back to your sister," I said. Both of them froze, but Flash didn't move to return the picture. "Now."

"She's being so annoying with it, though," Flash complained. He held the picture over the edge of the bed, and Lilly snatched it from his hand. It tore, leaving Flash still clutching a large piece.

I hadn't heard wails of anger like that since Lilly had first started her period several years earlier.

"You ruined it," she screeched, and made a lunge for her brother.

My mom finally bothered to acknowledge our existence and removed her headphones. "Would you mind? A woman can't think straight with the racket you two are making."

"Well, maybe if you would have intervened before it got to this point, it could have been prevented," I said, jumping up on the bed to form a physical barrier between the two.

My mom huffed. "Grandmas don't intervene."

"But they help their grandkids break and enter?" My breaths were coming heavy, and I realized it might be time for me to concede and allow natural selection to take over. It would be survival of the fittest, and hopefully I'd still have two children at the end of it.

"You act like it was a bigger deal than it was," my mom said with an exaggerated eye roll. "Flash and Lilly," she called over the noise. "Do you wish I would have left you home?"

They both stopped mid-fight.

"This is the best thing you've ever done," Flash said, sweat making his hair matt to his forehead. "I've never seen so much food in my life."

Lilly gave a vigorous nod. "And I wouldn't have gotten autographs from Ace Hutchins and Rachel Sinclair." She threw an annoyed glance at her brother. "Even if Flash did ruin one of them."

"Nothing that a bit of tape won't fix," my mom said. "But you're both making me look bad, and if you keep acting like a couple of toddlers, we'll need to head back home tonight. Is that what you want?"

"No, Grandma," they both mumbled.

She gave a satisfied nod, put on her headphones, and went back to her book.

"You could have done that when they first started fighting," I said, my breaths just starting to slow. If she heard me through the headphones, she acted like she hadn't.

I extended my hand toward Lilly, and she handed me the two pieces of the photograph. It was Ace's, and he'd written,

To my beautiful Lilly. May you continue to brighten the world around you.

His handwriting was impressively tidy for a man, his letters small and uniform. Even his signature underneath was legible. It had been ripped right between the o and the r in *world*.

Handwriting could tell you a lot about a person. Ace hadn't been in a hurry to sign yet another autograph. He hadn't been trying to get it out of the way—he'd taken his time. Made Lilly feel special. No wonder she was in love with the man.

And I wouldn't have been able to find any reason to worry about him, if not for Serena and Noah.

Now? I looked at the handwriting and saw a man who was careful. Calculating. Dangerous.

"May I see the photograph of Rachel Sinclair?" I asked.

Lilly was more than happy to show it to me, carefully lifting the picture from the desk and bringing it over to me. She kept her back to Flash as a defensive measure.

"Do they always keep photographs on hand, just in case?" I asked, taking it from Lilly.

"I guess," Lilly said, raising her shoulder. "When I asked for an autograph, I was just going to have them sign a napkin from the snack bar, but Ace went back to the dorms and grabbed these instead."

Rachel's wasn't personalized. And if I was correct, the signature had been pre-printed. She hadn't done a thing at all. It had even been Ace who'd gone back to the dorms to get the pictures.

"They're lovely," I told Lilly, and handed her the pictures. "You guys been here long?"

Flash swung his legs over the edge of the bed. "Naw. Dr. Randall came by the rec room about thirty minutes ago and said it was time to head to the dorms for the night, so we all left. He was wondering where you were, said he'd found your purse sitting outside the rec room."

Oh, yes. The purse that Serena and Noah had stolen. Sort of.

"Did he give it to you?" I asked.

Lilly reached under the desk and handed it to me. My gaze instinctively sought the button-like device that had been stuck on the inside lining. It didn't come as a surprise that it was now gone.

"Thank goodness," I said, masking my disappointment. "I can't seem to keep track of this thing today."

I hadn't liked being careful about what I said, knowing the sheriff was listening to everything. But it had also made me feel safe, knowing that even if she didn't hear what was going on, her deputy would.

I went to pull out my phone, but it wasn't in its usual pocket. In fact, nothing was. Almost like the purse had been dumped and the contents hurriedly shoved back in. Maybe in a search for another listening device.

The extent that Serena and Noah had gone to to hide their identities didn't sit right with me. Maybe they were just scared.

But scared of what?

Yes, there had been a murder, and Serena knew a lot of secrets as the resident celebrity psychic. She worried she'd be next. But I couldn't help but doubt the murderer had their sights on her, considering she was the murderer's fall guy. Without her, the sheriff would have to start looking other places.

"What is that?" my mom said, lowering her headphones. She nodded at the picture Lilly was still holding.

"Rachel Sinclair's autograph." Had she really not been paying attention to anything? Maybe she was in the beginning stages of dementia. I grimaced. That was a possibility I didn't want to consider.

My thoughts must have been written all over my face because my mom frowned and impatiently waved her hand at me. "I'm not talking about the autograph. I was there for it, remember?"

Yes, I did remember. I just hadn't been sure she had.

"On the back of it."

Lilly flipped over the picture, and written in small letters at the top was one word.

HELP.

16

The four of us stood clustered together, staring at that tiny word.

HELP.

"What do you think it means?" Flash asked from over Lilly's shoulder.

Lilly threw him an annoyed glance. "It means Rachel is asking us for help, genius."

I gave her my best mom look. "Be nice. Your brother's right to question it."

"You don't think she really needs help?" Lilly asked. "It says it all right there. HELP."

"But help from what?" my mom chimed in. "Or from whom?"

"And is it she who actually wrote it?" I added.

That last question grabbed everyone's attention.

"Why wouldn't she have written it?" Lilly asked. "You

think someone else would randomly write HELP on the back of her photo?"

I picked up Ace's picture from the desk. "No, not randomly. But maybe a person who was trying to protect Rachel when she refused to ask for herself."

Lilly took Ace's picture from me and studied them both, side by side. "You're right. It's Ace's handwriting. The small, uniform letters are a perfect match."

"So, the question is," I mused, "do I need to speak with Rachel, or is it Ace who needs conversing with?"

Flash was already bent over and lacing up his shoes but paused. "We're coming with, right? I mean, it's because of us that you even have those pictures."

"Actually, it's because of me," Lilly said.

"A joint effort," my mother so helpfully added.

I released a sigh of exasperation. "How's it going to look with the four of us traipsing around late at night and then accosting the celebrities? We don't even have access to their dorms. The plan is that I'm going to invite Rachel for an impromptu chat right after breakfast tomorrow so I can get to the bottom of this."

No one seemed to be listening to me. By the time I'd finished speaking, my family was already halfway out the door.

"We shouldn't be out here," I whispered, hurrying after them. "It's dangerous. Not only that, we're literally sleeping down the hall from the people who can fire me."

"Everyone is leaving tomorrow," Lilly said. "We don't have time to waste. Not when Rachel Sinclair needs us."

"But they'll all be asleep," I tried again.

Flash looked at his phone. "It's nine-thirty. No, they won't."

My kids stopped at the end of the hallway and peeked around the corner. Lilly waved us forward as if she were in a spy movie, then slipped out of view.

"This is your fault," I told my mom.

True to form, she merely smirked and said, "It's not my kids leading the pack."

"It's a waste of time and an unnecessary risk. We're sneaking around with a murderer still on the loose."

"Good," my mom said. "Then we'll have a better chance at catching him."

I released a low groan. "I really should have brought my purse." And then I remembered that the listening device was no longer there and we were on our own.

The kids had stopped and were waiting for us. Lilly raised an eyebrow. "Why do you need your purse?"

I'd also forgotten that they didn't know about that.

"My phone is in there," I said.

Flash held up his. "No worries, I have mine. Never go anywhere without it."

Spoken like a true teenager.

My footsteps slowed, even as theirs quickened. "I feel weird about this. Like we're being set up."

My mom glanced over as she passed me. "You're being paranoid."

That made me stop completely. "Paranoid?" I let out a disbelieving laugh. "A woman is dead. And I believe Whitney when he said that everyone is here for a purpose. On the inaugural flight, the astronauts didn't know each other. They were assigned according to the order of the waitlist. But this... This is different. Contrived. And no one feels safe. Why should we be any different? Who knows, maybe we're here for a purpose as well."

Lilly turned back. "And what if something happens to Rachel because we chose to hide under our beds and wait till morning?"

Now my own daughter was guilt-tripping me for trying to keep them safe. I'd been known to make less-than-wise decisions in the past when I'd thought it would help someone. But I didn't like it now that the tables had been turned. Now that my kids were following my lead.

I was about to put my foot down and be a good mom— demand they return to the dorm—when a shout came from the other end of the hallway. Running steps. Calls for the sheriff.

The kids didn't even glance at me when they took off toward the commotion.

I ran after them, my mom yelling from behind, telling us that her knee was acting up again. But my kids didn't slow down, which meant I couldn't either. Not with the uncertainty of what we were about to find.

My pulse quickened when we rounded a corner and saw Sheriff Potts sprinting through the doorway to the astronaut training pool.

I ran harder, hoping to catch the door before it closed behind her, but I wasn't fast enough. I skidded to a stop just as it closed. I didn't have security clearance for the training areas, and all I could do was wait.

That didn't stop Lilly from trying, her hands on her hips as her gaze traveled over the door. A narrow window ran along the top of it, and she motioned for her brother to come near. He put out a knee, and she clambered awkwardly on top while he attempted to keep his balance.

"Lilly, I don't think we—"

I didn't get the chance to finish my sentence. My daughter lost her balance and fell to the tiled floor, her eyes filling with moisture. At first I thought she'd been hurt. Until she spoke.

"They've pulled someone from the water, Mom." Her voice hitched. "I think it's Ace Hutchins."

"What did I miss?" my mom asked loudly, finally catching up with us. She leaned over and placed her hands on her knees, her breaths coming fast.

"Another murder," Danielle said, exiting the room. She wasn't in uniform, instead sporting gray lounge pants and a T-shirt, her hair pulled up into a ponytail. She gave me a look that said, *What?* when she caught me staring.

I averted my gaze. "Ace Hutchins?" I asked.

"Ace Hutchins," she confirmed, her lips tightening into a grim line. "With Charlotte I had no problem coming up with a list of suspects. With this guy, though–he didn't have an enemy in the world. America's heartthrob and voted nicest celebrity three years running."

Lilly was already nodding before the sheriff finished speaking. "When I asked for an autograph earlier, he went all the way back to the dorms to get his picture for me. Wrote a lovely message on it too."

Yes, he had been very good at portraying that image, but Serena's words stuck in my mind. These celebrities, including Ace, were the underbelly of Hollywood. What exactly had America's heartthrob done to obtain the success he'd achieved?

"Maybe you and I should have a little chat," Danielle told me, lowering her voice. When my mom and the kids perked up, she added, "Alone."

"But—" My mom started to protest, but the sheriff cut her off.

"There has been a second murder, and this one is much closer to home. You are all now confined to the dorms until further notice."

I nodded to the kids. "Do what she says. I'll be along in a minute."

There was more grumbling, but they shuffled along with my mom.

Danielle stayed silent as the emergency responders

entered the swimming area, a look of dejection mirrored in each of their faces. The sheriff's deputy stayed behind to take pictures.

"Dr. Harris will be along with his hearse, but it will take an hour for him to get here," she finally said.

"I suppose you'll be guarding the room until then?"

Sheriff Potts gave a single nod.

"Have any ideas who did it?" I asked after a long silence.

She gave me a side glance before returning her attention to the deputy. "I was hoping you might have something, considering you disposed of the device that was supposed to give us a leg up in this thing."

"That wasn't me," I said with a start. "My purse was stolen, and when it was returned to me, the device was gone."

Danielle gave me a rare smile. "I know. Just thought I'd see if you knew anything I didn't about that."

I wasn't in the mood to return her smile, though. Because my family and I had inadvertently been caught in something we didn't know how to get out of. And I was afraid to get any closer—to dig any deeper.

"Ace wrote a message on an autographed picture of Rachel Sinclair that she gave to Lilly. Just a single word," I said. "Help. We'd thought he was trying to protect Rachel —thought she was the one in trouble. I told the kids everything was fine and we'd wait for morning. They wouldn't listen. If we had been out here even five minutes earlier—"

"But you weren't, and judging by the state of Ace, he likely had been in that swimming pool for at least an hour. Maybe more."

I turned to the sheriff, angry. "That's not the point. I want to take my family home. It's too dangerous for them here."

She didn't react, merely folded her arms across her chest. "Understandable. Just tell me what went on in that room with the psychic, and then you are free to leave."

I gave a hesitant nod. "Fine." I glanced down the hallway. "But not here."

The sheriff extended her arm in the direction of my office, and I led the way. It wasn't until I'd swiped my badge and we were inside with the door shut that I felt safe enough to speak.

"Brace yourself, but Noah—he's Serena's brother. He was with her in the library."

Danielle nodded slowly. "Yes. Their father owns Galactic Enterprises."

I stared.

Her lips tilted up at the corner, like she was amused at my surprise. And maybe happy that she had known more about what was going on than I had, for once. "Don't look so shocked. I did some digging on the astronauts and anyone else who had the ability to get close to them. That, and David told me."

"David?" Who the heck was that?

The sheriff winced. "Officer Bridge. I am surprised he

allowed Noah in there with Serena, though. She wasn't meant to have visitors, even him."

I sank onto the couch. "If you dug into the astronauts' backgrounds, then you know how shady all of these celebrities are."

"I only know if they have a criminal history and what the media has released, as well as what documents Galactic Enterprises has on them." Danielle leaned against my desk. "If you're asking me if I know who has a grudge against who, I'd appreciate some enlightenment in that area."

I exhaled. "I don't know many specifics. But Serena claims she's innocent. Says that Charlotte was a week away from losing her business and that there's nothing left to inherit. It wasn't a motive for murder."

Danielle pursed her lips. "Go on."

"The only other thing she told me was that the celebrities here have all done terrible things to get where they are in their careers. Including Ace Hutchins."

It was quiet as the sheriff massaged her brows. "Ace ends up dead," she muttered, talking to herself. "It can't be Serena because she was in the library, guarded by Officer Bridge. Whitney has a lot of anger toward Ace, which certainly gives him motive. But what did he have against Charlotte?"

"That I couldn't tell you, though it seems that Whitney and Emma have a past. Maybe they dated and Charlotte didn't approve." I paused. "I'm not sure if this is relevant, but Officer Bridge left his post for at least thirty minutes, which is out of character for him. He said he had to request permission for Serena's therapy session, but he never returned, so I ended up letting myself into the library."

Sheriff Potts straightened. "You're kidding." She shook her head and muttered, "I knew David would be a complication. And my mother wonders why I don't date. It's hard enough to do my job properly without having to worry about this kind of stuff."

I tried not to let my shock show. My family had been right. Danielle Potts and Officer Bridge were romantically connected. Good for her. Except that it was causing problems.

"He wasn't outside the library when you arrived?" she asked, her gaze snapping to me.

I shook my head. "Or when I left."

She didn't bother with any more questions, instead hurrying from the office and heading straight to the library. I had to half-run just to keep up with her. When we arrived, Officer Bridge was sitting in a chair outside the entrance, reading a book. He glanced up, his brows popping up in surprise, as we rushed up.

"Hello, Danielle. Everything okay?" he asked, clumsily getting to his feet. His book dropped out of his hands, and he snatched it from the floor.

The sheriff's lips were pressed in a tight line, and she didn't seem to know how to answer that question.

He glanced at me, looking suddenly nervous.

"Everything is not okay," I said.

Danielle seemed to gain her bearings and said, "Open the door. I need to talk to our resident psychic."

17

Officer Bridge was at a loss as to what was happening. The sheriff was content to let him stew, not revealing why she was angry, only making certain he knew he should be worried.

He sent her nervous glances as he opened the door and gestured for us to enter.

I immediately scanned the room, half-expecting it to be empty. But Serena was exactly where she should have been, pacing like a caged cat. Noah was conspicuously absent.

"Mind telling me what's going on out there?" Serena demanded. "It sounded like someone was shouting from the other end of the spaceport, and I'm trapped in here and have no way out. Do you know how scary that is?"

Danielle seemed as surprised as I was that Serena was,

in fact, in the library as she was meant to be. "Um...yes. I mean, no. But I can imagine."

Serena looked between the sheriff and me. "Are you going to tell me what's going on, or..." Her words faltered. "Your energy. Something terrible has happened." She grabbed onto a chair and gripped the back of it so tightly that her knuckles turned white, and her words came out as a whisper. "Who was it?"

"Ace Hutchins," the sheriff said.

Serena's breath hitched, and she squeezed her eyes shut. She was silent, her eyes still closed, but she moved her head side to side, like she was looking at something. Or more accurately, searching. It was another minute before she spoke. "He didn't see it coming—trusted his killer." Her eyes flew open. "I may not have liked the guy, but he didn't deserve this. No one does."

"No, he didn't. Neither did Charlotte," Danielle said. "Which leads me to ask, where have you been for the past two hours?"

It seemed a silly question to me. Not the question itself, but actually expecting an answer. Serena had no choice but to say she'd been in the library the entire time, because that was where she was supposed to be.

"Right here," Serena said. "And some of that time can be corroborated by Dr. Swallows."

Danielle studied the psychic. "But not all of that time."

Serena hesitated. "No, not all of it."

"When did your brother leave?" the sheriff asked,

pulling out a notebook. When she saw Serena's surprised expression, she couldn't resist a sigh of frustration. "Why are people always shocked that I know what goes on around here? I do know how to do my job, and it was very brazen of the killer to think he, or she, would get away with murder when I was literally on the next hall over."

"Very brazen," Serena quickly agreed. "Noah left just after Dr. Swallows did." She then threw me a look of curiosity. And annoyance. She'd been surprised at the sheriff's question because she'd thought I'd keep that information to myself. She felt I'd betrayed her trust.

Danielle scribbled something in her notebook and then glanced up. "When did Officer Bridge return to his post outside the library?"

Serena raised a shoulder. "I have no idea. I've been behind a guarded door for half the day." She paused. "Sheriff, now that I couldn't possibly be the murderer, I would like to return to the dorms, please."

"You want to—" Danielle choked on an incredulous laugh. "That isn't happening."

"But there was no way I could have killed Ace. I've been here ever since you shut me in."

Danielle's smile disappeared. "Says you."

Serena released a frustrated groan. "Says everybody. Officer Bridge is always guarding that door."

There was no way Serena didn't know he hadn't been there. Not with Noah slipping in and out the way he had.

The sheriff gave her a hard stare. "Once I have a better approximate time of death, then we'll discuss this further."

She spun on her heel and walked out the door, leaving me, once again, hurrying after her.

"Officer Bridge," Danielle barked over her shoulder, not bothering to slow down. "That door will remain guarded, and you will not leave your post unless the deputy or myself is present, or so help me I'll make sure you never work security again. Anywhere."

"Y-yes, ma'am," he said, stumbling over his words. "Danielle. Sheriff Potts." When I glanced back, his complexion had paled and he looked like he might pass out.

I rarely saw the sheriff in this form, and it was terrifying. I opted to stay quiet, though I had no idea where she was leading me as we twisted and turned through the hallways. We were soon in a part of the building where I'd never gone.

Danielle stopped suddenly and knocked on a door to our left.

Whispering ensued, but I couldn't make out what the voices were saying.

"This is Sheriff Potts. You have five seconds to open up this door."

The whispering gave way to sounds of someone scrambling with the lock on the door, and soon after we were facing Rachel, with Emma standing behind her.

So, this was where the astronaut dorms were. They

were much nicer than the staff dorms, the beds made with beautiful blue sheets and a star-filled comforter. Even the lamps were themed, with the base shaped like a rocket.

"Is there a problem, Sheriff?" Rachel asked, blinking rapidly, as if we'd woken her. Considering it was just after ten o'clock, I wasn't buying it. Her eyes were red and swollen, and she wiped at them with the long sleeve of her robe.

Danielle stayed quiet and studied the singer for a moment. "You seen Ace Hutchins recently?"

Rachel scrunched her nose. It seemed she was trying to look confused but wasn't doing a very good job. There was a reason the woman was a singer and not an actress.

"Not since around seven-thirty. I was tired and came back to the dorms. Stressful day, you know. The highest of the highs, on our flight, and then the lowest of the lows when we returned. First Charlotte, and then—" Her voice hitched.

Emma stood silent and looked as if she'd like nothing more than to blend into the background.

"What about you, Emma?" I asked, and Danielle shot me a look that told me she didn't appreciate me interjecting.

Emma started at being addressed directly. "I—oh, I... I don't know. Ace left the rec room immediately after Rachel did. I stayed." She paused, and it was in that silence that I knew she wasn't telling us everything.

Ignoring the sheriff, I said, "Maybe you didn't see him after that, but did you hear something?"

Emma hesitated and looked to Rachel, who then nodded.

"Around eight o'clock, I heard arguing from the guys' room," Rachel said. "Someone stormed out. It was Ace. He said he was going to go for a swim. He does that when he's angry. Helps him calm down."

Danielle straightened. "Did it sound like one person or two left the dorm?"

"I can't be sure, but it sounded like it was just Ace."

Emma added, "Around that time, while I was in the rec room, I heard Julie talking to someone in the hallway. She told them that the pool was off limits for recreational use. It was only intended for training exercises. I didn't hear the person respond, but I did hear footsteps walking away."

"So, was Ace ignoring Julie, or was his killer the one who put him in the pool?" Danielle mused.

She pulled out her notebook and began scribbling, asking who they thought might have a vendetta against Ace as she did so.

As they talked, a black object protruding from under the bed caught my eye.

"Excuse me," I said, slipping around Rachel and Emma and into the room.

Emma spun around. "Hey, you can't—"

But it was too late. I'd already retrieved Jeffrey's camera and held it by the strap midair. "I've seemed to misplace a lot of things today," I said. "Including this camera. Jeffrey was frantic when he realized he'd forgotten it at the spaceport. He'll be forever grateful, I'm sure."

Emma opened her mouth to speak, but then closed it again.

That was probably a smart move.

Rachel, however, hadn't gotten the memo that she should stay quiet. "Are you here to accuse us of something?" she demanded of the sheriff as I exited their room with the camera in hand.

Danielle's gaze slowly panned between Emma and Rachel. "No," she finally said. "Just doing my due diligence, considering there have been two murders in the past twelve hours. I'm sure I don't have to tell you what this means."

"What exactly do you think this means?" Emma squeaked out.

Rachel answered for the sheriff. "That the murderer is still at large. And if they aren't found, we could be next."

Danielle gave a curt nod. "You are to stay in your room for the remainder of the evening. Either my deputy or I will escort you to breakfast."

We had turned to leave when Emma spoke. "Does this mean Serena is no longer a suspect?"

"It doesn't mean a thing."

And without further explanation, she left Rachel and Emma to stew on what she meant.

18

Danielle didn't waste any time when the dorm room door shut. "All these people are covering for each other, not worried they might be next. But they should be," she said as she walked swiftly down the hallway.

I struggled to keep up, fumbling with the camera as I walked. I wanted to know why those women were so interested in what was on this thing.

My breath caught in my chest when the picture that popped up on the screen was one I'd never seen. Before the camera had been stolen, an image of the astronauts standing in front of the spacecraft had always been the first to show, and I'd had to scroll past it to see older pictures.

Now, the most recent picture was of Lilly with Ace Hutchings in the rec room. It seemed this was the moment he was presenting her with his autograph. Lilly would love to have a copy.

But Jeffrey hadn't been here for that—he'd already left. Someone else had been taking pictures with this camera.

I was about to flip to the previous picture, but my attention was diverted when the sheriff stopped abruptly and held up a hand. I took it to mean *stay still and be quiet*. I didn't usually obey commands, but I did this time.

"The men's dorm," she said quietly, pointing to the door she'd stopped at. Only it was ajar, and shouts were coming from inside.

Danielle's hand rested on her gun, and she used a toe to push the door open.

I instinctively took a step back, just in case. But when the door came to a stop and I sneaked a peek inside, confusion replaced fear.

Whitney was on all fours, pulling what appeared to be a pile of clothes out from under the bed, and Noah was on the top bunk, throwing garbage into a bag that Flash was holding open for him.

My mom stood at the head of the room like a drill sergeant. "If you can't manage to take care of this tiny room for three days, I'd imagine your lives are in a similar state of chaos." She glanced over to where Whitney was shoving the clothes he'd discovered into his duffel bag. "Have some respect and fold those clothes like a proper man," she barked.

The helpless expression on his face—I felt sorry for him.

Lilly stood closest to us and noticed the movement from the doorway. Her eyes widened and she hurried out, partially closing the door behind her. "I know what this looks like—"

"I have no idea what this looks like," Danielle interrupted. "What possessed you three to come here by yourselves when one of those two could be a murderer? You do realize that we have another dead body, right?"

Lilly gave a little nod, blinking back moisture. I had a feeling it had less to do with the sheriff getting upset with her and more to do with Ace Hutchins being the person the sheriff had so callously referred to as *another dead body*, but Danielle mistook it as the former.

"I'm sorry. I didn't mean to snap," she said, softening her tone. "But I'm not happy about finding you three here. How am I supposed to question those two if your mom has them spit-shining their shoes?"

Lilly lowered her voice. "We're looking for evidence. Figured what better place to hide something you don't want found than a messy bedroom? Law enforcement is more likely to ask questions than rifle through garbage and dirty underwear. Besides, we weren't sure if you would need a search warrant to do that kind of thing here."

I glanced at the sheriff. It was genius, really. I could tell from her conflicted expression that she was both annoyed and impressed. I had no doubt that she'd been so busy running around the spaceport trying to do damage control, she hadn't had the inclination to search anyone's room. Hadn't seen the need. She had the murder weapon, after all. At least the first one. I wondered what the second was.

"It was Flash's idea—he hides stuff in his messy room all the time," Lilly said, looking proud of her younger brother.

Danielle's annoyance melted into amusement as she tossed me a little smile. "Tells me a lot about your parenting style and how the kids get away with so much, doesn't it?"

"I make him clean his room," I said, feeling defiant.

Danielle chuckled. "I wonder what you would find if you were the one to clean it once in a while."

I didn't like the direction this conversation had taken and gave a pointed look at the dorm room. "Shall we focus on the issue at hand?"

The sheriff's smile dipped. "Right." She opened the door once more, but this time made sure she made a show of entering the room. I followed her in, but a terrible smell nearly knocked me over, and I had to step back out and watch from the safety of the hallway. I didn't remember that smell from a moment earlier.

"As much as I appreciate you helping these men with improving their life skills," Danielle said to my mom, "I need you to return to your room."

The room had been transformed, only a stray sock resisting the impromptu cleaning.

My mom placed her hands on her hips and surveyed

her handiwork. "At least you won't die from the awful stench anymore. I sprayed some perfume I found in the bottom of my purse to cover up the boys' locker room ambiance they had going on. It smelled like wet dog."

I poked my head in and immediately pulled back. My mom's perfume had made the room uninhabitable. Those poor guys.

My mom exited the room, followed by my kids. Although my mom had a triumphant air about her, Flash and Lilly looked dejected. Must not have found the evidence they were looking for.

"Nothing?" I asked softly.

Flash shook his head. "They've only been here three and a half days, but you'd think they'd been here a month with the amount of dirty clothes and garbage we uncovered. And it wasn't even meant to hide anything. They really are just gross."

Even the sheriff didn't dare venture in too far. "Other than cleaning your room, where have you two been for the past two hours?" she asked Noah and Whitney.

"Been here," Whitney said, jutting out his chin.

Noah nodded and repeated, "Been here."

Danielle didn't write anything down. "Why did Ace go to the training pool? I'm sure you boys know that it's off limits for recreational use."

Both men shifted under her stare.

"Said he needed to cool off," Noah finally said.

Whitney scowled. "Dude, shut up," he murmured,

though it was loud enough for even me to hear from the doorway.

"You two have an argument or something?" the sheriff asked.

Whitney's glare intensified, and Noah stayed silent.

For a moment anyway.

"I lied," Noah said, the words bursting out. "I wasn't here the whole time. It was just before eight when Ace took off, and I left soon after to visit Serena in the library."

The sheriff leaned forward, her eyes beady. "And why did he leave in such a hurry?"

Noah hesitated, throwing an anxious glance toward Whitney.

"You do want to help Serena, don't you?"

Danielle knew the exact button to push, and when to push it.

"Ace had been saying that his whole world was crumbling around him—that he couldn't trust anyone," Noah said, ignoring Whitney's murderous glare. "Whitney reminded Ace that he wasn't exactly an angel—that he'd stolen movie roles from deserving actors. According to him, Ace had been willing to blackmail his way to the top. And Whitney had been one of the victims of stolen roles. Whitney said that Ace had..."

Noah hesitated.

"Had what?" the sheriff prodded.

Noah sucked in a long breath. "That he'd blackmailed Serena to get her to tell Whitney to turn down that movie role. The one that made Ace famous." He gave a quick shake of his head. "But I know that's a lie. Serena didn't have anything he could have used against her. She isn't the type. But just to be sure..."

"You went to see your sister in the library," I said.

All three heads swiveled in my direction, and they seemed surprised to see me, as if they'd forgotten I was there.

Noah nodded. "It was just before nine that I returned to the dorm room."

Whitney turned on Noah, incredulous. "Serena is your sister?"

Noah ignored the question and instead turned his attention to the sheriff. "Would it be all right if I slept in a different room tonight? Any room will do."

I could sense the anxiety behind the question. He was scared of Whitney—scared that he was the one who had killed both Charlotte and Ace. And Noah didn't want to be alone with him.

I didn't blame the guy.

Danielle didn't give Noah any special treatment, though. If anything, I thought she was being harder on him than the others. Maybe it was because of who his dad was. Maybe she was afraid of being accused of treating him differently. Whatever it was, she took her notebook out and began scribbling rather than answering.

"So...is that a no?" he finally asked.

Danielle finished writing her thoughts, then slipped the notebook back into her pocket. "That's a no."

"And if Whitney kills me in my sleep?" Noah asked, his voice rising several decibels.

The sheriff moved to exit the room but paused to say, "Then I'll make sure he gets life in prison." She glanced at Whitney, whose expression held a mixture of shock and anger. "Better make sure Noah doesn't die tonight. By your hand or any other. Your life depends on it."

19

To say that I was impressed had been an understatement. I'd never seen the sheriff so ruthless before. But it hadn't been cruel. More like she'd done it to protect Noah, in case he was in need of it.

She, however, didn't seem to think anything of it. Time was running out, and she had a one-track mind. "Any pictures deleted off that since you last looked at it?" she asked, nodding to the camera that swung around my neck.

"Uh, no, I don't think so," I said, turning it on. The picture of Lilly with Ace popped up. "If there were, though, I wouldn't know it. There are more pictures on the camera than when I had it."

Danielle raised an eyebrow. "More? You mean someone else has been taking pictures with it?"

"Yeah," I said, raising the camera so she could see the

screen. "This picture of Lilly getting Ace's autograph—I wasn't there, and Jeffrey had already left the spaceport. Someone else took it."

Danielle paused in the hallway and studied the picture. Other than Ace and Lilly, Emma and Whitney were the only ones in the photo. Emma was in the background, leaning against the snack bar with an amused expression as she watched. Whitney looked less amused.

"Flash?"

"How would the camera have ended up in the women's dorm room if Flash had taken the picture?"

Danielle didn't have a good answer for that. "All right. Not Flash." She nodded toward the camera. "What other pictures did our mysterious photographer take?"

There were two others, neither of them seeming to have any significance, though they all had one common element to them: Ace Hutchins. In the first, Ace was leaning against the wall in the hallway and reading a letter, his brows knit in concentration. Nothing too spectacular about that. In the second, Ace was dumping the contents of his suitcase on the dorm room floor, like he had lost something. At least that explained part of why the room had been in the state it was.

"Looks like someone had a stalker," Danielle said. "All of these are in public places, and the one with the suitcase appears to have been taken from outside the room, looking in."

Maybe. But there was another common element in each of the pictures, other than Ace Hutchins.

It was his expression. He wasn't smiling in one of these photos. When he held the letter, it was confusion. With the suitcase, it was anguish.

But the picture of the autograph worried me most. Because even as he was signing his name for my daughter, his expression was of fear.

I squinted and moved the camera closer. "This wasn't when he was signing his autograph," I said.

Danielle raised an eyebrow. "What do you mean?"

I removed the camera from around my neck and handed it to the sheriff. "This was when he was asking for help, hoping Lilly would see it. But she was too excited—too caught up in the moment. And an hour later, he was dead."

KNOWING that someone had been following Ace, the first place the sheriff and I visited was the security office to look at the video feed from the spaceport's surveillance cameras. The security officer there was unable to be of any help to us, however, because cameras had not been installed in this part of the building. He said he didn't know why and if we had additional questions, we could speak with Officer Bridge.

"David, why are there no cameras in these hallways?"

the sheriff asked Officer Bridge, speed-walking to where he sat in his chair in front of the library. "Or anywhere else, for that matter."

When he'd first seen the sheriff, Officer Bridge's entire face had lit up. Her deep-set frown seemed to have caused him to second guess himself, though, and his expression dipped into disappointment. "No need for them," he said slowly. "We have surveillance cameras positioned on the outside of the building and throughout the east end of the building where the spacecraft and our engineers are housed. All the classified stuff has state-of-the-art security. But honestly, we hardly use this portion of the building, except for the cafeteria. That will change when we have more flights coming through here, but currently, a few security officers and emergency personnel is all we've needed."

The sheriff released a hard sigh and shook her head. "That needs to change before your next flight."

Officer Bridge's lips pulled into a frown. "We're doing the best we can, Danielle. More information means more we have to track, and right now our sole focus needs to be the safety and security of classified material."

"More important than the lives of your guests?" Danielle countered.

Officer Bridge gave her a hard stare. "That's not fair. We had no way of knowing something like this would happen."

Danielle looked like she had more on her mind, but I didn't want to give her the chance to share it.

"Sheriff Potts," I said, placing myself between her and Officer Bridge, "I think it's time we focus on what we can control."

Officer Bridge stood from the chair and tucked his book under one arm. "I agree." And then he walked away from his post.

"Where are you going?" Danielle called after him.

"Serena is your suspect, not mine. I don't think she did it. So, I'm leaving her in your control so I can attend to my actual job—the one that matters. I only agreed to babysit her because I liked you. Thought it might help my chances when I asked you out for dinner after the investigation was over. Seems like it didn't work, though." Officer Bridge didn't glance back as he walked in the direction of the administration offices.

"Can you believe that guy?" she sputtered.

I gave her the side-eye. "Yeah. He's a good man, and a good officer. Takes his job seriously, like you. You two could have been a great team. But then you basically accused him of not caring about the lives of the astronauts. If I were him, I'd have walked away too."

Danielle stared. She was used to me talking back to her, but this seemed different. Like I'd struck a nerve. "My dog would be a better security officer than him," she finally said, though it was without conviction. Just a way to get in the last word.

Her dog. Of course.

I broke out in a run back toward the celebrities' dorm rooms.

"Where are you going?" she called.

I didn't bother answering.

20

W hen I arrived at the men's dorm room, Whitney answered after the first knock, as if he'd already been standing there.

My breaths came fast as I said, "It smells like wet dog in here. That's what my mom said. You have wet clothes in here." I gasped, pulling in another breath. "From falling into the swimming pool."

Whitney's face paled. "You're wrong."

I shook my head and leaned against the doorframe so I wouldn't pass out. "No, I'm not. And I'll go over every inch of this room if I have to. But I'm going to prove that you were in that swimming pool with Ace Hutchins just before he died."

Danielle pushed past me, not at all out of breath. "I'll do the honors."

Noah scrambled to the opposite end of the room,

looking as if he'd like nothing more than to not be trapped with the sheriff.

"Fine," Whitney said, his tone panicked. "Yes, we'd gotten into an argument. Yes, I'm jealous of his success. And yes, I'd suspected he'd done questionable things to help launch his career. But I felt bad about the things I said and went to the training pool to apologize. I've never had any proof that he's done me wrong. I overreacted."

"But then when you saw him, all of that anger resurfaced. Am I right?" Danielle asked, pulling a lump of wet clothes from under the blankets of one of the empty bunks. My mom hadn't thought to look there. Now I knew where I should have hidden the things she hadn't approved of when I was a teenager.

Whitney shook his head. "No. By the time I got there, he was already in the pool, face down. I used to be a lifeguard and thought I could help him, but..." His voice broke.

I believed him.

The sheriff wasn't as easy to convince. "When you realized you wouldn't be able to save him, you what, put him back in the pool? How convenient just in case we find Ace's blood on these clothes."

"Blood?" I'd assumed that Ace had drowned. No one had said anything about blood.

Whitney gave a small nod, and he paled further. "He had a big gash on his head. Like he'd been hit with something."

"A crime of passion. Grabbing the first thing at hand," I murmured.

Danielle nodded. "Yes. A crime of passion. And Whitney had plenty of that."

His gaze snapped to her. "Maybe I did. But that doesn't mean I killed him. As much as I resented Ace, I'd never do something like that. I respected him. Not that I'd have ever admitted it to his face."

The sheriff grunted as she exited the room, wet clothes in hand. "We'll see about that."

The moment she was clear of the door, it slammed shut.

"You're going to find Ace's blood on those clothes," I said.

She nodded. "I know."

"But I don't think Whitney did it."

Danielle released a dejected sigh. "Neither do I. But what choice do I have? I need to hold Serena for Charlotte's murder, and Whitney for Ace's. That's where the evidence points."

I scrunched my nose, forcing my mind to focus.

It didn't cooperate.

If only the killer would be kind enough to send us a signed confession, it would make this so much easier.

I paused. Maybe they had.

I snatched my phone from out of my purse but moved so quickly, it went flying out of my hands and skidded across the hallway.

"You okay?" Danielle asked, her gaze curious as I scrambled after my phone. "You thought of something, didn't you?"

"Hope so." Flash had the audacity to not answer until after the fourth ring.

"Did you find a letter in the men's dorm room?" I asked without so much as a hello. That letter Ace had been reading—it had to be somewhere. "Probably addressed to Ace."

It made sense that that had been what Ace had been looking for amongst his things—why he'd dumped out his suitcase. He'd probably tucked it in there so others wouldn't stumble upon it.

"Depends on who's asking."

I groaned in frustration. "Now's not the time, Flash. Was there a letter?"

"Yup, mixed in with a pile of clothes under the bed. Looking at it right now. Whoever wrote it really went out of their way to mask their handwriting. Seriously, we're going to need to get a professional in here to decipher this thing."

My breath hitched. "And you didn't think to tell me the moment you found it?"

"We wanted the chance to look at it before you took it away," my mom yelled from the background. "Which I know you will."

She was right, of course. I would be taking that letter.

"From what little we can read, it's a threat," Flash said.

"Ace had stumbled upon the truth of how Charlotte died, and the killer wanted him to know that no good would come of him going to the authorities. They offered Ace a good deal of money to stay quiet, but either Ace refused, or the killer didn't trust Ace to not take the money and still turn them over to the authorities."

This murderer was ruthless and covering all their tracks. Which meant my family was in danger just being in possession of that letter.

"Flash, you three need to stay in that room and not open the door for anyone. I'll be right there."

I hung up, not allowing him the chance to argue.

"What's wrong?" Danielle asked.

My pulse raced, and I felt jittery. We were close—I could feel it. But I wondered if the murderer could feel it as well.

"I need you to call all of the astronauts into the library for an emergency meeting," I said, my gaze meeting hers. "We're flushing out this murderer tonight."

21

My kids weren't happy when I took the letter from them and then forced them to stay in our dorm room. My mom was furious.

"That's the thanks we get for helping you?" she said. "You're always happy to take what we uncover, and a little gratitude would be appreciated. Instead, you lock us up until you need us to perform again."

I stood my ground. "For starters, I didn't ask you to organize and clean the men's dorm and I never ask you to perform. But I am about to enter a room where there is at least one murderer, so forgive me for not wanting to place my family into that kind of environment."

"You're not forgiven," she huffed. "But you're right, it's much too dangerous for children."

She'd actually listened to me. That was a first. But then she turned to the kids.

"If we're not back in thirty minutes, something has gone terribly wrong, and you need to call Benji for help."

Nope. I couldn't do this. Not now. I'd rather risk hurting my mom's feelings than risk her life. She might stop talking to me for a while, but she couldn't hold out forever. She loved her grandkids too much.

As my mom was slipping on her shoes, I hurried out the door and took off running. I couldn't force her to stay in the room, but I also hadn't told her where I was going.

It wasn't until I neared the library that I allowed myself to slow to a walk. I didn't want to appear like a complete lunatic, after all.

Emma and Rachel entered the hallway from the opposite end, and my breathing hitched. Danielle was trusting me by gathering everyone together, but what if I was only going to embarrass both her and me? And put my family in further danger. I only had one chance to get this right—what if I was wrong?

I forced my breathing to slow. That was why I was gathering everyone together. So I could read the room. Not the way Serena claimed to do with her psychic powers. But really read the room. Observe who was avoiding eye contact with whom and see how people reacted when others spoke, or when I asked questions.

Basically, I was about to have the largest group therapy session I'd ever done.

When I entered the room, the tension was so thick, it made my skin crawl. It was awful. But it was exactly what I needed. If I was this on edge, so was everyone else, times a hundred.

From a quick scan of the library, I noticed that Serena and Noah were sitting on opposite sides of the room, still not wanting others to know their true identities. Julie, Officer Bridge, and Dr. Randall must have caught wind of my plan because they stood against the bookcase in the back, seemingly wanting a vantage point where they could observe the entire room. Didn't want any surprises.

Whitney was sitting on one end of the couch in front of me with Emma on the other.

That left Rachel, who moved to a high-backed chair next to Noah.

The sheriff entered behind me and took a quick count of the attendees, her head bobbing as she counted each. "Good, you all made it."

"Didn't really have a choice, now did we?" Whitney grumbled. His shirt was inside out, which meant he'd probably dressed in a hurry. I glanced at my phone. Eleven o'clock.

"What's with the theatrics?" Rachel asked, looking far more put together than the last time I had seen her, though I could still catch a glimmer of moisture in her eyes.

"A last-ditch effort to pin the murders on one of you," Serena said from her side of the room.

Whitney scrunched up his nose. "Why one of us? You

must be their prime suspect, otherwise you wouldn't have been in solitary confinement all day."

"I requested it so I wouldn't have to deal with you," she shot back.

Danielle held up her hands. "Okay, folks, let's play nice. Dr. Swallows has a few questions she'd like to ask, and you will give her your full cooperation." She gestured for me to take over, but as she did so, she leaned in and whispered, "You better know what you're doing."

"The psychologist?" Emma said with a laugh. "This should be good. You going to get us to talk about our feelings, hoping one of us will slip up and confess?"

I smiled and stepped forward. "Something like that."

And then I didn't say anything more, instead watching reactions. Rachel leaned back in her chair, looking both exhausted and annoyed. Probably had a crying-induced headache. Whitney rolled his eyes, while Noah closed his, as if he were going to take a nap.

Serena was the only one who looked interested in what I might have to say. She leaned forward, her elbows resting on her knees, and held my gaze. Her eyes were bright, like she couldn't wait to see what would happen next.

That left Emma, but she'd perfected her poker face, and I couldn't read her expression. Bored, maybe. Or indifferent. But considering I was there to catch her mother's killer, neither made sense.

"Seven astronauts went up into space. Six came back alive," I started. Now, everyone avoided eye contact, including Serena. "I've been having trouble imagining what happened up there, and I need your help."

I began moving chairs so they resembled the arrangement of the seats on the spacecraft. Everyone on board had a window seat, so there were two chairs on each row with an aisle separating them. I was short two chairs and motioned for Noah and Rachel to move so I could use theirs. They stood, though reluctantly.

"A reenactment," Whitney said, folding his arms over his chest. "This is a waste of my time." He turned to leave, but Sheriff Potts moved in front of the door, blocking his exit.

I rested my hands on one of the chairs. "Charlotte was sitting in the last row at the back of the spacecraft. Emma, you were across the aisle from her." I motioned for her to come take a seat. After a quick glance around the room, she complied. "Directly in front of Charlotte was Serena, with Whitney as her neighbor across the aisle."

"She wasn't killed while we were all seated, though," Emma said, taking her seat at the back of the makeshift spacecraft. Whitney sat down in front of her. "I would have known. It had to have been when we were all floating around."

"Says Charlotte's sole heir," Whitney muttered.

He didn't know that Emma wouldn't be inheriting anything.

I nodded to Emma. "I think you're right. The murderer likely came up behind her. A knife was found under the seat directly in front of Charlotte. Serena's seat. But everyone was flipping and floating through the air, so no one saw anything. Or so they say."

Rachel's gaze snapped to me. "If you found the knife under Serena's seat, and it's obvious you already suspect her, why aren't you arresting her and putting an end to all of this madness?"

The sheriff spoke up. "Because it would have been easy for anyone to slip the knife under the seat with its close proximity to Charlotte."

Serena threw a glare in Rachel's direction. "Besides, why would I put it back under my own seat? That would make me stupid."

"Well, if the shoe fits," Rachel said, suddenly very interested in her cuticles.

Serena moved to stand, but the sheriff gave her a look that would have made me pee my pants.

Serena sat back down.

"Emma," I said, placing my hands behind my back and taking a step toward her. She shifted in her seat, looking uncomfortable at being under the spotlight. "You told the sheriff your mom never alerted anyone that she'd been stabbed. Never asked for help. It wasn't until the return flight that she started complaining of pain in her side."

She gave a little nod. "Yeah, and she was always complaining about something hurting. We'd been to the ER three times in the last four months. They said it was anxiety."

"That must have been difficult," I said.

Whitney snorted. "Or just another cry for attention. Charlotte couldn't get enough of it."

Emma's nostrils flared, and I jumped between them before she could do anything she'd regret.

"Let's say it was anxiety. The doctor said it was possible that she didn't even feel the knife enter, due to adrenaline from the flight." I paused. "It can't be easy as a fashion icon, always worried about keeping your place at the top."

Emma nodded. "You have no idea. I know people say I was mooching off her as I worked on my career, but the truth was, she was a very fragile woman. She relied on others more than she wanted to admit, and it made her feel vulnerable. My mom hated that she needed me, so she compensated for it by being harsh and unforgiving."

"How did her temperament affect the fashion empire she'd created?"

Emma's expression turned to one of fear as she eyed the others in the room. If she showed any sign of weakness, the others would use it against her.

"I'm not trying to be mean," I said, my voice quieting. I crouched next to her chair so only she'd be able to hear me. "But there is a very complex dynamic happening in this room, and I need to understand it. If not, your mother's death may go unsolved, as will Ace Hutchins'."

Emma's eyes teared up. "So, you don't think I did it?"

I hadn't been sure until this moment, but I went with

my gut instinct and shook my head. "No, I don't believe you did."

In an even quieter voice, Emma said, "The business was going great. Until recently. But my mom had gone through some tough financial times a few years back, and she was forced to bring in a silent partner." She hesitated. "Ted Carson. He's been receiving sixty percent of the business's profits, which is robbery, if you ask me. He took advantage of my mom's desperation. But at least she was able to retain control. He only wanted the financial benefits, a piece of the pie, if you will."

"But?"

Emma blew out a hard breath. "But sales slumped last year, and this year wasn't looking any better. My mother's dresses are—were—still the choice for awards ceremonies, important events and that kind of thing. But my mom needed Ted to invest more money. Just a little until things picked up again. He told her that she'd be fine if she wasn't so picky about who she worked with. She got angry. Said it would hurt the brand if she worked with any random celebrity who flashed money at her. Ultimately, Ted refused to invest any more money. He said my mom's era had ended and he wanted out."

I was beginning to understand. "She was about to lose it all." Serena had mentioned that the company was about to go under. She hadn't mentioned her father was the cause of it.

"How did she afford your flight tickets with how poorly business was going?"

Emma wiped at her eyes. "She bought our tickets years ago. We've been on a list, waiting for flights to open up."

My legs started cramping up from squatting so long and I slowly stood, stretching them out. It was no surprise to find the others leaning in, trying to catch our words. Serena had moved from her chair at some point and was now positioned closest to us. Judging by her guilty expression, she'd heard every word.

"Is that why your dad sent you and Noah?" I asked Serena. "To foretell Charlotte's demise?" Serena opened her mouth to protest, but I held up a finger. "I should clarify, the demise of her company."

"Like I said, he swears he had nothing to do with us being here," she said, though her gaze was darting all over the room. She couldn't stand to look at me. "We were on a waiting list and he said he'd move us up to the next flight if we ever decided to come. But he didn't make the call."

"Then how—" Oh. I had been overlooking the obvious. "Charlotte found out who her favorite psychic really was. The daughter of her silent partner. She thought your father was exerting control over the company through you—that he wasn't being as silent as he ought to be. Charlotte must have been angry, considering that she listened to your predictions as religiously as if they'd come from a higher power."

"Yes, she was angry," Serena said. "Wouldn't believe

that I had no idea my dad was a silent partner in her company. He is very good at the *silent* part of things, particularly when it comes to his children." Her eyes flashed. "She kicked me out of her house and threatened to tell everyone I was a fraud. But that was weeks ago, and my being here has nothing to do with Charlotte."

I saw now what Dr. Randall had meant when he'd said he'd seen her claws come out. This was a woman who knew how to survive.

"I disagree," I said. "Your being here has everything to do with Charlotte. You still don't know who arranged for you to come on this little trip, do you?" I turned away and walked down the aisle of our spacecraft to the next empty chair and looked at who we had left. "We haven't filled our flying vessel yet. If I'm not mistaken, it was Ace Hutchins in front of Serena and Rachel.

Just the mention of Ace's name sent Rachel into another fit of tears.

"I know it's difficult, but I need you to take your place," I said kindly, and gestured to her chair.

"I don't know why she's so upset; it was my best friend who died," Whitney said.

I glanced at him. "Yes, but it was her boyfriend. And you didn't even like him."

Every head whipped toward me, and Rachel stumbled as she walked.

Whitney snorted and threw the sheriff a smirk. "You

sure this is the shrink you want helping you? She hasn't gotten anything right so far."

Rachel's expression told a different story. I nodded to the chair. She had regained her composure, but her eyes were wary as she walked toward me.

"How did you know?" she asked, her voice shaking.

Emma shook her head with an exasperated sigh. "I can't believe I didn't notice before. You sneaked out every night after the rest of us were in bed, always acting like you needed the restroom. But no one is ever gone that long. Even on a bad day."

"Why keep something like that a secret?" Serena asked Rachel. "If I were dating Ace Hutchins, I'd be shouting it from the rooftops."

Whitney's smile was gone. "Maybe she was embarrassed because he wouldn't allow them to be seen together."

"You're just jealous because you've been hitting on her the entire time and she hasn't given you the time of day," Serena said with a laugh.

"Publicity," Noah said, speaking for the first time since we'd all gathered. "There are rumors he's dating his costar from his current film, and it's helping the hype. Movie doesn't release for another three months." Every head whipped toward him, shock etched in their features. "What? I pay attention sometimes."

Rachel gave a weak nod and collapsed into the chair. "I suppose it doesn't matter now that he's..."

More tears.

I pulled up the empty seat that would have been Ace's and sat with her, allowing her to grieve. I had the feeling it made the others uncomfortable, just sitting in silence as Rachel cried. But she hadn't been allowed to grieve properly—had had to hide how deeply it ran until now.

"I'm curious how you knew," she finally asked through her tears.

Danielle hurried over with a box of tissues, and I took it from her, offering one to Rachel. "I didn't realize it until today—you two were very good at hiding your feelings for each other. When he moved out of your way so you could see past him on that first day, I just thought he was a kind person."

"He was. Even if we hadn't been dating, he still would have moved," Rachel said before blowing her nose into the tissue.

"Even so, when my daughter asked for your and his autographs, he hurried back to the dorms to retrieve both his and your official photographs. I'm assuming yours was in your suitcase, and no man would rifle through a woman's belongings unless they were very close. Or dating." I hesitated before adding, "I noticed that your autograph was pre-printed, and his wasn't."

"You're asking if I care less about my fans than he does? Why I can't be bothered?" Rachel asked. I was unsure if I was meant to answer that, and thankfully she pressed on. "At events, I do sign them, or at least pretend to. Because I do care, and I don't want others to think otherwise. I pretended with your daughter as well. But my handwriting is horrible, and my manager insisted we have a computer-generated signature on each of my photos. Everything in our business is a show, including the simplest of tasks."

"But what do you do if someone randomly asks you on the street?" I pressed.

Rachel lifted her chin in defiance. "I sign it, because the fans don't care what my signature looks like, and it's no excuse to be rude." She then released a shuddered sigh. "Can you please move on to someone else? I didn't kill Charlotte—not over a dress. And I absolutely did not kill Ace."

I hesitated. "I'm sorry, but I have to ask one last question. Was it you who stole Jeffrey's camera?" Rachel looked like she was going to deny it, so I hurriedly added, "There were pictures of him that Jeffrey didn't take. And the camera was in your dorm room."

Rachel exchanged a side glance with Emma. "Ace had been acting weird. I thought he might be up to something."

"Weird, how?"

"On edge. Nervous. I thought—I thought he might be cheating on me."

I stood slowly and moved Ace's chair back to its position. "You never suspected he might have had something to do with Charlotte's death?"

Rachel's hands clenched into fists and her eyes narrowed. "Never."

I agreed with Rachel. Ace didn't kill Charlotte. But I did believe his change of behavior had everything to do with her death. "The last one left is Noah. Can you take your place, please?"

With everyone in position, looking nervous, I paced the library. Serena was positioned in front of Charlotte on the spacecraft, making her seat an easy place to stash the weapon.

Ace was in front of Serena, meaning that, despite the astronaut exploring the entire spacecraft in microgravity, he may have seen when the weapon was replaced.

But how had the weapon gotten on board in the first place?

Flashbacks to the first day at the spaceport.

My gaze whipped to the group in front of me.

I thought I knew who had killed Charlotte. I just didn't know why.

And then my mom burst into the room.

22

"It was Rachel," my mom shouted as she burst into the library.

I supposed that was one way to do it. Even though it was absolutely the wrong way.

Rachel jumped to her feet, her face ashen. "Lies. That woman is crazy. I could never hurt either of them."

The energy in the room escalated, everyone talking at once. Danielle rushed to my mom and tried to get her to leave, but she wasn't having any of it.

"Mom, what are you thinking, barging in here like that? You have to leave," I said, joining the sheriff.

My mom huffed and folded her arms over her chest, clearly telling me she didn't intend to go anywhere, at least not quietly. "I picked up a woman's butterfly hair clip in the men's dorm room when I was helping them clean—it clearly didn't belong to one of them. And shortly after you left, I remembered where I'd seen it before. In that picture that Rachel autographed for Lilly. Rachel was wearing it." She paused and gave me an accusatory look. "Of course, then it took a full fifteen minutes just to find where you'd gone."

"Ace and Rachel were dating," I said. "It doesn't prove anything, and now you've completely upended everything I've been working toward."

My mom's lips dipped into a pout. "I was only trying to help."

I pulled in a deep breath and reminded myself that helping was all my mom was ever trying to do when she interfered with my job, my family...my life. But trying wasn't enough when it came to a murder investigation.

"Mom, thank you for coming down here with that additional information, but..."

My mom didn't seem like she was listening, her gaze instead scanning the room. "Of course, Rachel wouldn't have written that threatening note. A woman's messy handwriting is different than a man's. Not sure why men's is always worse. With the exception of Ace, of course. Beautiful handwriting."

Frustrated and realizing I wasn't going to get my mom to leave without a fight, I sat down on the sofa, needing a think.

"Noah, what is your connection to Charlotte?" I asked, thinking aloud.

The room quieted, and he looked around at everyone, nervous.

"There isn't one. I've never met the woman," he said.

"And you, Whitney?"

Whitney squirmed in his seat. "No connection between Charlotte and myself. Emma and I dated a couple years ago, but Charlotte didn't think I was good enough for her daughter and refused to be in the same room as me. Never had so much as a family dinner."

I'd been so clueless, trying to tie everyone to the fashion icon. Give everyone a motive. But it wasn't she that everyone was connected to.

"Not everyone in this room personally knew Charlotte," I mused. "But everyone knows Serena. Whether they admit it or not, they've turned to her psychic readings to further their careers. She's the common thread in all of this."

Silence.

Serena's expression turned panicked. "Yes, I know everyone here. So what? It's not a crime."

"And you're in Charlotte's will. Or you were."

Serena was looking downright terrified now.

"But the knife was hidden under her seat," Noah said quickly, beginning to sound equally scared for his sister. "She wouldn't do that."

I nodded, feeling more confident about the trajectory of my thoughts. "You're right. She wouldn't. But you would."

Noah's lips parted, but it was another moment before sound escaped them. "What are you talking about?"

"Did you search Noah when boarding the spacecraft?" I asked Dr. Randall, my words slow.

All eyes turned to the former astronaut, and he looked decidedly nervous at everyone's attention on him. His gaze dropped. "No. I knew he has sensory sensitivities. Touch being one of the most severe for him. It was the reason he chose not to participate in most of the training activities."

"That and I didn't want to be here in the first place," Noah muttered.

I turned back to Noah. "I've noticed that you keep yourself at a distance from everyone else, and not just because you don't like them. Sensory sensitivities are common among those who have dyslexia. So is particularly terrible handwriting. Like in the letter you wrote to Ace, threatening him."

"I didn't threaten him," Noah said.

I continued, knowing I needed to press harder. "You must have been relieved when, after my mother said your room smelled like a wet dog, Whitney fessed up that he'd jumped into the pool to try to save Ace. That meant we wouldn't go looking further. If we had, I'm fairly certain we'd have found a second set of wet clothes. Did you go to the swimming pool with the intention to kill Ace?"

Noah was now near tears, shaking his head vigorously. "Why couldn't he just let it go?" he whispered. "Charlotte was horrible. Evil. I overheard her talking with someone on the phone the morning of the flight. Telling them that she'd managed to strike the fear of God into my father by arranging for Serena and me to be on the flight. That she was showing him who was the one in control and that she was going to deliver the fatal blow before we left the next day. I didn't know what that meant, but she was determined to bring my dad and his entire enterprise down, just like he was trying to do to her. Only she was going to make sure she did it first."

I moved closer, one slow step at a time. "I thought you didn't think much of your family. You were estranged from both your father and sister, weren't you?"

Noah gave a small nod. "But that doesn't mean I'm going to allow someone to hurt them. It wasn't until the flight when I found my opportunity. If only Ace hadn't seen. I thought for sure that he'd tell Julie or Dr. Randall. Or the sheriff, when she arrived. But he didn't. It was like he was waiting for something. And it paid off. When I told him who my dad was…well, that was a mistake. Ace didn't want money for his silence—he already had plenty of that. Once he knew how powerful my family was, he thought he could leverage that. He wanted some of that power."

"You weren't going to allow someone to hurt us, and yet you killed Charlotte and tried to pin the blame on me," Serena yelled, launching herself at him. The sheriff caught her just in time, pinning Serena's arms behind her.

Noah sprang to his feet. "Of course not. The best way to ensure you wouldn't be under suspicion was to plant the knife in such an obvious place. No one would be that dumb."

"Well, they apparently thought I was," Serena spat out. But then her expression softened. "Did you really do everything to protect the family?"

Noah nodded. "A lot of good that's going to do, though. Dad will probably be ruined after this. Your career will be finished as well, considering you couldn't even predict that your own brother was a murderer."

"I doubt that," Emma said. She'd moved from her chair and now leaned against the counter, snacking on pistachios. "You've just made your family more interesting. And enough people have paid large sums of money to reserve their seats on future flights, I doubt they're going to give it up that easily. I believe your dad has a no-refunds policy."

Sheriff Potts moved forward and placed handcuffs on Noah. He glanced back just as they reached the door. "I enjoyed our chats, Dr. Swallows. Thanks."

And then he was gone.

Julie, Officer Bridge, and Dr. Randall began to follow, but I stopped them as they were leaving.

"I've been thinking about how Charlotte managed to get Noah and Serena here this week. She'd obviously been planning revenge of some sort, whether it was blackmail or something more nefarious. But she shouldn't have had the ability to get them on this flight. Or any of the other celebrities, for that matter."

Julie gave a slow nod. "I've been wondering the same thing. As has Ted Carson."

"Maybe she paid someone here to move the travel roster around a bit," I mused. "It probably seemed a benign way to get their hands on a lot of money. Didn't see any harm in it."

Officer Bridge was already shaking his head. "No one here would do that. No matter how benign it seemed. Ted Carson has always treated us well, and we wouldn't betray his trust."

My gaze traveled to Dr. Randall. "I noticed you have a nice car in the lot. Is it new?"

Dr. Randall held my gaze but didn't respond.

"I'm assuming you don't make a lot of money here as a retired astronaut," I said. "It's especially painful when you're having to deal with entitled celebrities that now get to be called astronauts. What a slap in the face." I paused. "How much did Charlotte pay you to move up a few departure dates? One-hundred thousand?"

"Three-hundred thousand," Dr. Randall whispered.

Julie blanched. "Oh, Fred. Are you serious?"

"Charlotte knew her company was going under," I said. "Might as well drain the business account for a worthy cause—enacting revenge."

Officer Bridge's brows furrowed, and he seemed to be struggling to gain control over his emotions. After an uncomfortable minute, he grabbed Dr. Randall's arm.

"We're going to have a chat with the sheriff and see what she wants to do with you."

A thick silence settled over the room as the three of them left. All except for the sounds of Rachel's tears. She was sobbing, still seated, head buried in her hands. When I approached her, however, she waved me away.

I turned to Emma, expecting to see at least a hint of tears, now that we'd caught her mother's murderer. There was nothing.

"What happens for you now?" I asked her.

She raised a shoulder. "My mom apparently thought more highly of a bunch of dogs than she did me. Maybe I can find some money hidden in the mattresses before I'm kicked out of the house. Seems like the type of thing she'd do."

"What a terrible thing to say," my mom said. I'd forgotten she was still with us.

"She was a terrible mother. Did I wish her dead? No. Did I wish for her money? Yes. And since that isn't happening, I have to make the most of what I'm left with."

My mom turned to me as we walked from the room. "In case you think you're getting an inheritance, there won't be one. Just warning you now not to get your hopes up."

I snorted. "Worried that the kids and I will kill you for your garden gnome collection?"

Before she could confirm or deny, my kids came running down the hallway. "Grandma locked us in the dorms. Stuck a wedge under the door from the outside," they shouted in unison.

"Mom," I yelped. "What if there had been an emergency and they couldn't get out?" I swung my gaze to the kids. "How *did* you get out?"

"Noah let us out," Flash said.

I exchanged an alarmed look with my mom. "But he's—"

"The murderer," Lilly said. "Yeah, we know. He apparently made a run for it but paused long enough to kick the doorstop out when he heard us banging. Nice guy, all things considered. We caught the tail end of things as the sheriff was tackling him right outside the room."

I blew out a hard breath. "It's weeks like this that remind me why the world needs therapists."

"Speak for yourself," my mom quipped.

Unfortunately, I had been.

23

I wasn't even given the chance to pull my suitcase out of the back of the car before Trish burst out of the house, ran across the lawn, and tackled me in a monstrous hug.

"Please, never leave me again," she said, refusing to release me from her death grip. "Even before your mother kidnapped the kids, she stopped in at least three times a day to make sure I hadn't endangered their lives. Heaven forbid I cook homemade pizza."

"And it's a good thing I did," my mom said, stepping out of her car. She'd insisted on following me home to make sure the kids and I made it safely. "The smoke alarm was going off when I arrived."

Trish released me, and I could tell she was fighting her natural instinct to argue with my mom. I knew the feeling well. She settled for pursed lips. "The smoke alarm always goes off. Every single time we use the oven."

Home sweet home.

I gave her a smile. "At least you were able to get some quiet time while the kids spent the night with me at the spaceport, right?"

Trish laughed. "Sure. Except, Benji called me every ten minutes because he didn't want to bug you at work, so he bugged me instead, asking if I had any information on what was going on out there. Honestly, you could have at least called him to let him know you were alive."

"I did. I talked to him at least twice a day. Three times yesterday."

Benji walked out of the house just in time to hear me, sweat on his brow and his tool belt secured around his waist. Looked like he'd finally gotten a long enough break from work to fix my baseboards. One of the many perks of dating a handyman.

"And it still wasn't enough," he said, moving behind me and wrapping his arms around my waist.

"Oh, gag," Flash said, walking quickly past us so he didn't have to watch.

Lilly followed closely behind. "Yeah. What he said." And then they disappeared into the house.

I smiled and twisted enough to give Benji a quick kiss on the cheek. "Well, we're alive, the case is solved, and now we can relax."

He released a long breath in my ear. "If only."

I turned in his arms to face him. "What do you mean?"

"Town council is up in arms about the development

that's happening downtown. They had a meeting two nights ago and are determined to stop anyone that comes to Amor looking to purchase the local shops."

I laughed. "That's nothing new. There's been talk of development for months. Ever since the inaugural space tourism flight, we were told we'd start to get high spenders traveling through here. Everyone that goes out to Galactic Enterprises spends a night here in Amor before heading out to the spaceport. Naturally we'll get some nicer hotels, restaurants, and everything that goes along with that."

"The meeting was bad, Maddie," Trish said. "Worse than usual. Carlos Herrera warned Mayor Freedman that if he didn't put measures in place to prevent the desecration of our town, the council would have to step in and do it themselves."

That gave me pause. "Since when do you go to town council meetings?" Ever since the council had accused her of spreading disease and destruction and threatened to strip her of her residency—she'd had the flu and gone to the pharmacy to get medicine—she had sworn off anything to do with the town council.

"Since they posted a notice on our door that if I didn't attend the meeting, they'd have no choice but to assume I was a co-conspirator," she said, her lips dipping into a frown. "I can't decide which is worse, dealing with your mom or them."

My mom harrumphed. "I'm still here, you know."

Trish gave her a smile to let her know that she was very aware.

"Carlos and the rest of the council are all talk," I said. "They'll do their best to pass ordinances and the like, but when it comes down to it, it's the business owners that have the choice whether to sell or not."

Benji stepped back, and his arms fell away. I immediately missed his touch. "Normally I'd agree with you. But Trish is right. It felt different. Carlos seemed almost... violent. He acted as if we were facing invaders and it was our duty to protect our home. Our families. Even Bob was looking uncomfortable, and you know how much he resists change." He paused. "Some of the other council members looked like they could be swayed."

That wasn't good. Thankfully, the mayor's sister was on town council, and Bob worked in the mayor's office. That should be enough to keep Carlos in line.

I picked up my suitcase with one hand and took Benji's hand in the other. "That's a worry for another day. Today, I'm just grateful to be home with you, where I don't have to worry if a murderer is on the loose."

"With your record?" Trish asked, following us inside. "It won't take long."

I should have knocked on wood.

The End

CHOOSE YOUR OWN ADVENTURE: MYSTERY OR ROMANCE

MADDIE SWALLOWS MYSTERIES

Dead Before Dinner

Dead Upon Arrival

Dead Before I Do

Dead Among Stars

Dead by Design

BORROWING AMOR: New Mexican Romance

Borrowing Amor

Borrowing Love

Borrowing a Fiancé

Borrowing a Billionaire

Borrowing Kisses

Borrowing Second Chances

STARLIGHT RIDGE: Beach Romance

Diving into Love

Resisting Love

Starlight Love

Building on Love

Winning his Love

ABOUT THE AUTHOR

Kat Bellemore is the author of both the Borrowing Amor small town romance series and the Maddie Swallows cozy mystery series. Deciding to have New Mexico as the setting for these series was an easy choice, considering its amazing sunsets, blue skies and tasty green chile. That, and she currently lives there with her husband and two cute kids. They hope to one day add a dog to the family, but for now, the native animals of the desert will have to do. Though, Kat wouldn't mind ridding the world of scorpions and centipedes. They're just mean.

You can visit Kat at www.kat-bellemore.com.